THE LEGACY SERIES

Fugitive Daydreams
Leah McCormack

Hoist House: A Novella & Stories
Jenny Robertson

Finding the Bones: Stories & A Novella
Nikki Kallio

Self-Defense
Corey Mertes

Where Are Your People From?
James B. De Monte

Sometimes Creek
Steve Fox

The Plagues
Joe Baumann

The Clayfields
Elise Gregory

Kind of Blue
Christopher Chambers

Evangelina Everyday
Dawn Burns

Township
Jamie Lyn Smith

Responsible Adults
Patricia Ann McNair

"Marie Zhuikov's *The Path of Totality* is a gem of a collection. These speculative stories explore a wide range of unusual situations with humor and insight, with empathy and heart. Readers will get carried away—just like these memorable characters get carried away—into imaginative worlds full of mystery and wonder. She delves into our longing for connections, how we respond in the face of strangeness and mystery beneath the ordinary."

—JIM RAY DANIELS
author of *The Perp Walk*

"Richard Powers meets Gabriel Garcia Márquez in a collection that nonetheless could have been produced only by a singular sensibility—one firmly planted in a fully recognizable, verifiable natural world that's also brimming over with mystery, wonder, and the fantastic. I love Marie Zhuikov's brain. She's both a scientist and a dreamer. These stories, rich in emotional metaphors that play out in magical ways, remind us to tread carefully and to always pay attention."

—SIGURD BROWN
author of *The Girl in Duluth*

"These stories concern everyday people discovering who they now are as opposed to who they once were. A grieving couple come to accept the death of their child. A woman pays too large a price for caring about a neighbor's son. And in 'Bog Boy: A Northern Minnesota Romance'—a gem of a story, a perfect story—a teen falls in love with someone suspended in time. Not all of Zhuikov's characters find peace and harmony, for the damned soul and the broken heart and the heart's longing are nothing to fool with. But the few who find love, for instance, Sheila and Peter in the long final story, enter paradise."

—ANTHONY BUKOSKI
author of *The Blondes of Wisconsin*

The Path of Totality

Stories & A Novella

Marie Zhuikov

CORNERSTONE PRESS

UNIVERSITY OF WISCONSIN-STEVENS POINT

Cornerstone Press, Stevens Point, Wisconsin 54481
Copyright © 2025 Marie Zhuikov
www.uwsp.edu/cornerstone

Printed in the United States of America by
Point Print and Design Studio, Stevens Point, Wisconsin

Library of Congress Control Number: 2024948517
ISBN: 978-1-960329-70-7

Cornerstone Press titles are produced in courses and internships offered by the Department of English at the University of Wisconsin–Stevens Point.

DIRECTOR & PUBLISHER
Dr. Ross K. Tangedal

EXECUTIVE EDITORS
Jeff Snowbarger, Freesia McKee

EDITORIAL DIRECTOR
Ellie Atkinson

SENIOR EDITORS
Brett Hill, Grace Dahl

PRESS STAFF
Paige Biever, Sam Bjork, Mai Kao Hang, Karlie Harpold, Gwen Goetter, Allison Lange, Sophie McPherson, Kylie Newton, Hannah Rouer, Ava Willett

to Logan & Hunter

CONTENTS

The Path of Totality

The problem with Justin Kincaid's eyes began on August 21, 2017. On a dusty hillside in Oregon, the curve of the moon's shoulder nudged away pieces of the sun. The crowd of people hurried to don their cardboard eclipse glasses. But to Justin, the sun still shone as whole and bright as ever.

Marjorie stood beside him. Through the background noise of the gathering, he heard her say, "It's a third of the way gone! Isn't that cool?" Despite his confusion, the excitement in her voice warmed something in him. She hadn't been enthused about anything in the past two months.

Justin turned his head from the sky and flipped up his glasses. Marge's pale face was lifted to the sun like an offering. She drank in the last of the warmth. Her long red hair—noticeably oily these days—was swept back from her face, tendrils falling over her shoulders.

He flicked his glasses back on and looked up again. "Yeah, amazing!" His heart beat a little faster. He hoped he sounded convincing. Why wasn't he seeing the eclipse? Something must be wrong. He rubbed his eyes behind the glasses.

This trip to the eclipse's path of totality had been his wife's idea. Marge said she needed a change of scenery. So, they drove early on that August morning from Medford to Salem, Oregon. Craig and Betty, a young couple who had recently begun working at the bank Justin managed, stood beside them on the hillside.

The two couples had driven separately and arranged to meet at a rest stop along the way. As Marge and Justin approached the bathroom building, a woman pushing a stroller walked out, followed by her partner. Justin walked past but looked back to see Marge stopped outside, staring at the child. Her arms were crossed over her wrinkled shirt, her face stricken.

The parents glanced at Marge and hurried on. After a few moments, when Marge still wasn't moving, Justin sighed and went to her. He gently touched her arm. "C'mon Marge. It's okay. Come inside."

She let herself be led into the building, turning back once to watch the retreating couple. With one hand on her elbow, Justin guided her to the women's restroom. He let her go and was relieved when she kept walking in on her own.

When Justin came out of the men's room, Marge was already out in the common area, talking with Craig and Betty. After exchanging pleasantries, Craig left the women and took Justin aside. Six feet, four inches, Craig looked down, slightly bending his lean frame. "Is Marjorie okay?" He hesitated and then added, "She seems distracted and looks kind of…"

Justin knew what it must have cost Craig to say this. In the short time they'd been working together, he'd noticed that Craig always tried to be positive, especially to him, his boss. Still, Justin was embarrassed that Marge's condition was so obvious. "She's just having a rough go of things lately," Justin said. "Marge needed a change, and the eclipse is a good distraction. She's been looking forward to seeing it so she can tell her students. This funk is only temporary." He didn't want Craig to know the real reason for Marge's mood. They weren't close enough friends for that.

Justin hoped Marge could return to her job as a substitute science teacher. It worried him that she didn't just bounce right back. He wasn't used to that. Staying home gave her more time to dwell on things, which didn't seem productive. She used to like making elaborate desserts while listening to classic jazz. Now their home was silent and even the store-bought cookies were running low.

Justin pulled his thoughts to the present. Until he could figure out what was wrong with his eyes, he should probably offer some comment on the eclipse. "How far gone do you think it is now?"

"Oh, at least fifty percent!" Marge said, still enthused.

Justin took off his glasses and looked around at the scattered crowd to see if that helped his vision. Maybe his eclipse glasses weren't working. Maybe his retinas were already burned beyond repair. Everyone was rapt, looking up at the sky. He could see the people just fine.

Betty chirped, "It's getting darker."

Justin ran his hand nervously through his black hair. This eclipse spanned from Oregon on a path to South Carolina. Fourteen states in total darkness, the first time an eclipse covered such a wide swath of North America since 1918. How could it be that he wasn't seeing it?

Marge took off her glasses, too, and looked up the slope. "Do you feel that? It's like a cold wind is blowing down the hill."

Justin *could* feel that. He could smell grit in the breeze. Was the light changing? Maybe. He might need to make an eye appointment. He put his glasses back on.

After more time passed, Craig said, "Ninety percent! Hey, look at the shadows on the ground—they're so sharp!"

The others moved their arms around, playing with the shadows.

"Oh my God, this is so weird!" Betty wriggled in delight, her brown hair bobbing.

Marge tapped Justin's arm. "Look around, just try looking around!"

He couldn't escape. Lowering his head, he raised his glasses again. In the crowd, people were sharing glasses with those who didn't have any. Some wiped tears from their eyes at the wonder of the sky. Justin moved his arms and looked at the ground just for show. "That's so cool!"

But it wasn't. He saw the same sorts of shadows that accompanied him any day the sun was shining. Sweat trickled down his armpits while an emptiness grew within.

After a few minutes, a slow cheer began to rise from the crowd, as if they were all at a football game, the moon a player running for the end zone.

"What the …?!" Marge held her glasses with both hands.

Beside Betty, Craig said, "Oh my God! What is happening?!"

The crowd laughed and started to clap.

Marge pointed to the town below. "Look! The streetlights are coming on."

Now the cheers of the crowd gave way to widespread and indistinct exclamations. Justin could only assume people were seeing the luminous circle of light from the blocked sun. Dammit, why couldn't he see the corona?

Craig took off his glasses and the rest of their group followed suit. He pointed his in a long arc. "Look at the sunrise, it's in every direction!"

Justin looked around with everyone else, plastering an expression on his face that he hoped would pass for awe.

"I don't know what I expected," Betty said, "but it wasn't this! It poked a hole in the sky. It's so dark."

"This just looks so wrong! The sun really is coming up on every horizon. It's so incredibly beautiful . . ." Marge's laughter gave way to deep breathing. A few children in the crowd were shrieking in delight.

Now Craig pointed into the sky. "Look, it's Venus! I can see stars, too."

Justin heard crickets begin to chirp. Relieved that he could contribute something real, he mentioned the sound.

Marge spoke more softly than before. "Oh yes, I hear them, Justin. We are inside totality."

Totality didn't last long. Soon, Craig said, "There it is; the sun!"

Many in the crowd started to cheer and applaud. Everyone put on their glasses again.

For a few more moments, the group marveled at the sun's return—long enough for Justin to suspect the day must surely be as bright to everyone else as it had been to him the whole time. The others started taking off their glasses. Justin removed his, too. "Let's eat, I'm starving," he said, desperate for a distraction.

The four walked over to their picnic basket and sat on a blanket they had spread out earlier. As he sat, Justin scanned the crowd and saw that they, too, were returning to their regular concerns, as if a spell had been broken. His heart began to slow.

Craig looked at his watch. "Well, if you guys leave soon, you could be home before dark." He gave a laugh. "Regular dark, that is."

Betty finished a bite of her sandwich. "This experience was so cool I almost don't want to leave."

Marge sighed. "Me neither."

Justin thought about what awaited them—a four-hour drive with just the two of them in the car, avoiding talk about anything meaningful, back to a silent house; back to a garage full of boxes they hadn't had a chance to move to the nursery.

When he came home from working late, sometimes he would find Marge standing in the dimness and dust, whispering the brand names like a mantra: "Graco DuetSoothe Swing, Modern Baby Nest Crib, Baby Bjorn Quilted Cotton

Bouncer Bliss, Bristol Bassinette …" Other times, he'd find her sitting in the middle of the box pile, huddled as if in a womb herself.

Maybe they should stay on this hillside.

Marge continued, "I'm ready to get home. I don't know about you guys—I feel like someone flipped a reset switch inside me."

A bit of the old glow lit her eyes. She had already eaten half her sandwich and was eagerly opening a bag of potato chips. Justin was glad she seemed to have her appetite back and he hoped this lasted. Maybe the drive home wouldn't be so bad.

"I . . . we feel pretty great, too." Betty looked to Craig. "You want to tell them?"

Craig's smile was broad as he gazed at Marge and Justin. "We just found out, and we'd like you to be the first to know—we're having a baby!"

In the moment it took Justin to respond, he remembered everything: the panic in Marge's eyes as her contractions started in bed. Even though they weren't sure what to expect with their first baby, they knew that at twenty weeks, those kinds of contractions were way too soon. He rushed Marge to the emergency room where the doctors tried to stop her labor, but it was too late. Her pains came harder and faster. An "insufficient cervix" they had called it. Andrew, their baby boy, had come too soon into a world that was too big and too cold. On the hillside, Justin glanced at Marge before he spoke. She was looking away, her eyes focused on something in the distance. "That's great, you guys!" Justin said. "You must be so excited." All the hope he'd been feeling started to drain away. He said a little prayer: *let Marge take this all right. Please!*

Betty bubbled, "Yes, a whole new world is opening up for us!"

Marge was still looking away. Justin said, "Hon, isn't that great for them? Hon?"

As if with great effort, Marge slowly turned back to the conversation. Her eyes glistened with moisture. "Yeah. Yeah, that's great. When are you due?"

"Next April," Betty said.

"That's my birthday month." Marge's voice was wistful.

"What day? Wouldn't that be great if it was the same?" Betty took an enthusiastic bite of her sandwich.

Marge took a deep breath and smiled. "Yeah, that would be cool. My birthday is the sixth."

After packing the remains of their lunch, the group sauntered to the bottom of the hill toward their cars.

Betty walked next to Justin. "You're awfully quiet," she said, peering at him. "What's up?"

"Just takin' it all in," Justin lied. "The eclipse and now this. It's big news. I wish you guys the best."

Promising to get together again soon, Craig and Betty climbed into their blue Honda to visit Craig's parents in Salem.

As Justin started the engine of their car and pulled out of the lot, Marge said, "Wasn't the eclipse awesome? I can't wait to tell the kids at school about it."

Cautious, Justin settled on, "Does that mean you feel like you could go back to work?"

"I think so. I feel so liberated." Marge gestured to the sky out the window. "I mean, if the sun can disappear and reappear, I ought to be able to deal with this and keep going." Her hand rested on her belly.

"I'm so happy to hear that." Justin patted Marge's leg as he turned the car onto the highway. "I was a little worried when Craig and Betty shared their big announcement." As he drove, Justin visualized Andrew in his incubator, covered with an oxygen tent to help him breathe. His chest rose and fell in a quiet battle for air. Wires coiled around him like snakes.

"That was hard," Marge said. "But you know what? Life goes on. I can't keep wallowing. I'm stronger than that."

Justin gazed at Marge for a moment. "Damn right, you're strong. And I'll help." He turned his attention to the car's speedometer. As he set the cruise control, he dared ask, "Do you think it would be helpful if we visited him?"

Marge didn't need to ask who he was talking about. Her eyes grew large and thoughtful. "I . . . I don't know." She hesitated. "Let's just go with this feeling for now and not rush things."

This was progress, finally. On the rest of their drive back to Medford, their conversation flowed much more easily than on the drive out. During the occasional silences, Justin thought about Andrew. Despite their parents' objections, he and Marge had decided against a funeral. They didn't want to spread the sadness around. Justin had taken care of the burial arrangements to spare Marge.

Andrew was buried in one of the local cemeteries—the one with the ponds where the ducks liked to swim. A friend said it was peaceful there, but Justin had never visited the grave. Neither had Marge. They didn't even put a headstone on it.

He could visualize the map that the cemetery lady had drawn for him—a red pencil line leading from the entrance to where Andrew was buried—the number of his metal grave marker written in the margin. Justin had filed it in the small cabinet in their home office.

During the following days, Justin's vision seemed all right, but in his dreams, he kept hearing an owl hooting, low and haunting. He wandered from room to room in his mind but couldn't find it. Finally, he went into the back yard, only to realize the hooting had morphed into a baby crying in the distance. The moon in his dream eclipsed the sun, only the sun never returned. Darkness was total and bleak. He'd awaken to Marge shaking him, asking if he was all right.

Part of him knew the owl was Andrew, but he couldn't tell Marge what was wrong. She finally seemed like her old self. She started showering every day and her hair was clean and shiny again. She even went back to work. He didn't want to mess that up. He, on the other hand, dragged himself out of bed every weekday morning. On the weekends, he slept until 10:30 a.m., which was unusual.

After a few weeks of this, he came home on a Friday night to find candles on the table and dinner waiting. Benny Goodman's clarinet music wafted from the speakers. He laughed in delight, not brave enough to ask about the occasion.

Their conversation was easy through dinner. Marge waited until dessert to ask, "What's wrong, Justin? I'm worried about you."

Justin slowly chewed the homemade turtle cheesecake for a while, letting the caramel melt on his tongue. He thought back to the nightmares. "I think it's Andrew."

"What about him?"

Justin rubbed his hands over his eyes. "I think we need to visit his grave."

Marge hid her face in a fall of her hair. She swept it aside.

He reached across the table for her hand.

She took his hand in hers.

SATURDAY DAWNED CLEAR AND WARM. They stopped at a flower shop to buy a spray of baby's breath and blue irises. With Justin driving and Marge consulting the red pencil line on the map, they drove under the cemetery's arched gate.

Justin maneuvered slowly down the narrow asphalt paths between headstones. They passed a pond with white geese and green-headed mallards clustered along the shore. A few people walked their dogs among the headstones and a maintenance man drove a riding lawnmower on a hillside.

They reached a big Douglas fir growing in the center of a turning circle. Marge pointed to the side of the road. "This looks like it. Let's park here."

She climbed out of the car and led the way, still holding the map. Justin followed, carrying the flowers, the musky scent of the baby's breath hovering around him. His free hand shook slightly.

He remembered how the nurses let them hold Andrew. He looked so peaceful; his bluish lips and closed eyes, his featherweight body so still. Justin had peeled off a few squares of monitor foam tape that were still stuck to Andrew's thin parchment skin as silent tears flowed down his face. Those were the only tears Justin had shed. After that, it was like they dried up.

Marge looked up from the map at a spot on the lawn where the earth had been disturbed between two large headstones. "Is that it?" They walked over and Marge bent down, feeling the soil for the small round marker. She brushed dirt away and looked up at Justin. "Yes, it's the same number." Then she sat back and stared at the impersonal silver marker glinting in the sun.

Justin dropped to his knees beside her. He peered at the marker and laid the flowers beside it. He turned to Marge. "You okay?"

The tears glistening on her cheeks answered him.

Justin sat and put his arm around her shoulders. The two of them started rocking side to side. Justin felt a liquid bubble rise through his heart. Slowly, it continued upward through his throat and into his head where it burst, releasing all the sorrow and loss he'd been pushing aside for so long. He choked back a sob.

"It's okay." Marge's voice was shaking. "You need to feel it, too."

They both cried all their tears. Wiping his eyes, Justin noticed a new sheen to everything, as if a film had been washed away. The grass was greener, the flowers on the graves more colorful. The air was crystalline, like after a summer rain.

As he blinked to test his new vision, his mind flashed back to the eclipse. With each blink, he saw the sun as it should have been on that hillside in Salem, blocked by the moon. Blink by blink, chunks of it disappeared.

He kept his eyes closed longer. In fast motion, pinpricks of stars appeared as the eclipse blocked the light and then allowed it to return. He fought dizziness as a replay of multiple sunrises beamed from every direction.

Sitting by the grave, Justin could finally see what everyone else had on that dusty hillside. Blazing orange and deep purple light washed over the dark behind his eyes, as if a hundred smokeless wildfires burned on the horizon. He gasped.

Marge asked, "What's wrong? Is something wrong with your eyes?"

Justin opened his eyes and turned to Marge, smiling and holding her. The physical contact steadied him. After a long moment, he replied, "No, my love. I see more clearly than I have in weeks."

Dedicated to my parents, who I wish had visited the grave.

Catfished

When live cod were shipped to Asia from North America, the fish's inactivity in their tanks resulted in only mushy flesh reaching the destination, but fishermen found that putting catfish in the tanks with the cod kept them active and ensured the quality of the fish.

—Wikipedia entry on "Catfished"

VIEW PROFILE

Username: WillYouBeMine
I am: Male
Looking for: Female
Desired Relationship: Marriage, long-term dating, long-distance relationship, pen pal
Age: 42
Zodiac Sign: Capricorn
My match age: 30–45
Location: United States, Boston
Ethnicity: Mixed
Height: 5'8"– 5'11" (171–180 cm)
Weight: 241–260 lbs (110–118 kg)
Body Type: About average
Hair Color: Brown
Eye Color: Brown

Status: Widower
Occupation: Supplier
Religion: Catholic
Do you have children: 1
Do you want children: It's okay if my partner has children,
Not sure I want more kids
Languages: English
Education: Master's degree
Income: $70,000–$100,000
Smoking: Never
Drugs: Never
Drinking: Socially
Pets: Dog
Favorite book: Island by Alistair MacLeod
Movies: Action and romance
Music: Slow and jazz

Essay:

I would appreciate a person who has a sense of who she is and a sense of direction about what she wants to achieve. I want a woman who sees a man as a friend and partner. I know that men and woman all have an inner child and that is why I would enjoy days filled with fun and laughter. I respect and adhere to taking care of business in life—family, work, community, etc. Yet I know life involves balance.

I'm an optimistic person and always look for the good in others. I know that life involves give and take and that people must be willing to give and demonstrate themselves to others. I am a romantic at heart. I like to be appreciated and complimented, and I would do the same for that special someone. I don't care much about age or about distance because age is just a number and distance is a space that can be covered. All I believe in is real love.

I would like someone who will love and respect me for who I am. Someone who likes to hold hands and surprise me with a little kiss when I least expect it or give me a wink from across the room. Or who will call me just to let me know she's thinking about me, because I will do the same. I would also love someone who is fun to be around, likes to laugh, joke around, enjoys being outdoors going for long, romantic walks, enjoy looking at the stars at night, and watching the sun set and rise over the ocean.

I am looking for someone who enjoys the simple things in life, just as I do. I would like to meet someone special who I can grow old with. My hope is we can look into each other's eyes and know that the love between us is just as wonderful and exciting as the day we met.

VIEW PROFILE

Username: Sarah1042
I am: Female
Looking for: Male
Desired Relationship: Marriage, long-term dating, long-distance relationship, pen pal
Age: 40
Zodiac Sign: Aries
My match age: 35–45
Location: United States, Madison
Ethnicity: White
Height: 5'5"– 5'8" (165–172 cm)
Weight: 125–140 lbs (57–64 kg)
Body Type: About average
Hair Color: Blond
Eye Color: Blue
Status: Divorced
Occupation: Administrative
Religion: Methodist

Do you have children: 2
Do you want children: It's okay if my partner has children,
Not sure I want more kids
Languages: English
Education: Bachelor's degree
Income: $40,000–$70,000
Smoking: Never
Drugs: Never
Drinking: Socially
Pets: Dog
Favorite book: Outlander by Diana Gabaldon
Movies: Drama
Music: Jazz and alternative rock

YOU HAVE MAIL
To: WillYouBeMine
From: Sarah1042
May 16, 2014

Hi,

I like your essay. I haven't had time to do an essay yet because I just joined this site. Your photo is attractive. Feel free to look at my profile and see what we have in common.

OUTGOING MAIL
From: WillYouBeMine,
To: Sarah1042
May 17, 2014

Wow, you are pretty, Sarah! I love everything you said about yourself on your profile and that means you are interesting to be with and beautiful. It's been a while since I joined this site and I haven't found anyone yet. My name is Christopher Edward. What's your middle name? Tell me about yourself. Have a wonderful weekend. Chris xoxoxo

YOU HAVE MAIL

From: Sarah1042
To: WillYouBeMine
May 17, 2014

Hello Chris,

Thanks for your reply. Today's going to be busy for me, so I thought I would reply while I have a moment. My name is Sarah Ellen. I'm an administrative assistant at a university. I see from your profile that you are a "supplier." What do you supply? Not drugs, I hope! 😊 I also see that you have a child. How old is he or she?

I have two sons and I own a dog (a labradoodle). What breed is your dog? Like you, I like reading and movies. I'm a romantic at heart, also. I own my home, like to keep active, and still have all my teeth. 😊

I've been to Boston a couple of times. I like it—it doesn't feel like a "scary" city to me like New York or Miami. I'm a Wisconsin girl, you know.

That's all I have time for now. I hope you have a great weekend!

Sarah

MARCO INHALED THE PUERTO RICAN breeze coming through his kitchenette window. It carried the salt scent of the ocean from ten kilometers away. He walked a few steps to the table in his living room that also functioned as a dining room. He sat and began scrolling through his cellphone contacts, selecting his neighbor, Vinny. He answered on the second ring. "Did you finish editing my message yet?"

"To which girl?" Vinny asked.

"To Sarah. I'm putting Valerie on the back burner for now; she's getting too demanding. All her whining and questions. 'Why can't we meet? Why do I need to send you more money? Why didn't you call?'" Soon he'd have to cut loose the red-haired grocery store checkout girl from Wyoming.

Vinny chuckled. "I had to give my brother a ride. His car broke down in the middle of nowhere. I'll work on the message tonight. Can't keep your little cheesehead waiting, can we?"

"*Cheesehead?* Why'd you call her that?"

"That's the nickname for people in Wisconsin. Marco, I know you watch football. You tell me you've never seen the Packers?"

"Oh . . . yeah. It's just been a while. Why would I pay attention to them?"

"Well, if you got a fishy on the line from Wisconsin, you might need to," Vinny said. "What made her bite, ya think?"

"Probably the photo. Gets them every time."

"Which one?"

"The tough guy with the cherry tree in the background. Makes them think I'm a serious man with a soft heart."

Vinny laughed. "You're so bad! But hey, if it keeps money coming into my house, I can't complain. What was the 'tell' you put in this time?"

"I said I was 5'8" and weighed 240 pounds. Do I look fat in the photo? No. A smart woman would be tipped off. If she's dumb enough to miss that, it's not my fault if she believes everything else I tell her. I stole the essay from some sap on a different dating site. I've had good luck with it. Plus, women fall for the widower status—another pity card to play."

Vinny snickered. "You didn't put the Harry Potter books for your favorites, did you?"

"Nah, I wanted to attract older ladies with more money. I had to class up my style. I looked at a list of best books of the twenty-first century and chose *Island* by Alistair MacLeod."

"Oh, I don't know that one." Vinny muffled the phone and then came back quickly. "Hey, I gotta go. Cassandra needs me for something in the bedroom."

Now it was Marco's turn to snicker. Then he said, "How you ever got her, I have no idea, my friend."

"Well, you better be glad I did. Her connections help you and me both."

"Don't forget to send me Sarah's email edits," Marco admonished. "I don't know how much longer I'll need you for this one, but there's always the others."

"Right." Vinny clicked off.

OUTGOING MAIL

From: WillYouBeMine
To: Sarah1042
May 18, 2014

Hello Pretty Sarah,

How was your night? I hope you had a wonderful rest. You know what? My late wife's name was Ellen, just like your middle name. I love that name, but unfortunately, I don't have a daughter to name after my wife.

Wow. I find it difficult to take my eyes off your profile picture because you're so beautiful. I love your blond hair. You have two sons, right? How old are they and what are their names? I have a son who is ten years old, but he's not living with me. He moved to Australia to stay with his grandma after the death of his mother. She died in an auto crash in Madrid, Spain.

Ever since then, the family has been fighting with me, poisoning my son's mind against me, saying that I killed his mother—saying I was the cause of her death. Is it a crime to care, love, pamper, and spoil your wife with gifts, cash, and trips? I loved her and cherished her so much. I was only doing that because I adored her, and now she is gone.

Yes, I have a dog, too. He's a great dane, but he's not living with me. There's nobody to take care of him when I'm gone for work. My vet loves him and offered to take him, so my dog is living with him.

What do I do? I'm a building contractor and also a supplier. I supply security gadgets of all kinds for conference halls, hotels, malls, plazas, government, houses, etc. My work is interesting because I travel a lot and meet a lot of people both home and abroad.

I don't smoke and I don't do drugs. I am pure of heart and I live a good life, so you have nothing to worry about my Sarah Ellen. I have been single since the death of my wife. I haven't seen the kind of woman I want for myself or one who will take the memory of my late wife out of my head and make me love again. I have gotten over the shock, but I need a woman who will put a smile on my face. She should be a serious-minded woman and someone who will love me for who I am, not what I am. A woman who is loving and caring woman, kind, interesting to be with, intelligent, hard-working and trustworthy. No games.

I am a cool and serious-minded man who knows what I want. I believe in love and think that is what a relationship should be built on. As time goes by, you will get to know more of me. Ok? Enjoy the rest of your weekend with your sons.

Chris xoxoxo

YOU HAVE MAIL
From: Sarah1042
To: WillYouBeMine
May 19, 2014

Dear Chris,

What a sad story you have told me about your life. It sounds like you lost everything you love because of a car crash—your wife, your child, and later, your dog. Not to dwell on painful memories, but I find myself wondering how long ago it happened. And why does your wife's family think you are the cause? Of course, it's no sin to pamper your wife, but were you driving the car that crashed or something? It sounds like you loved her very much.

You asked about my sons. My oldest is twenty and doesn't live with me anymore. He's in college and moved out last summer on his own. My youngest is fourteen and he's finishing his last year in middle school. He's not very talkative, but he's smart, likes soccer, and plays trombone in band. My boys don't give me any trouble and I'm so proud of them.

Your work and life sound interesting. I'd like to think mine are, too. But I have no one to share them with. I've been divorced for over three years. During that time, I met two men in my town who I adored, but the relationships ended for different reasons. The first one was too old for me. Although, as you say, age may just be a number, it does sometimes relate to health once a person gets old enough.

The second man ended up losing his job and didn't feel like it was fair to be in a relationship without one. I didn't agree. I loved him for who he was, not what he did. But his identity was so tied up in his job that he couldn't function, so we aren't together anymore. However, we are still friends.

I'd like to think that I am a naturally happy person. My friends say I'm creative, yet down-to-earth, smart, and a great listener. I'm looking for someone who is good at communicating (you are certainly good at messaging!), romantic, likes having fun and traveling.

Well, I need to run out the door. Have a good day, handsome!

Sarah

OUTGOING MAIL

From: WillYouBeMine
To: Sarah1042
May 20, 2014

Hello Lovely Sarah Ellen,

How are you doing? I hope you had a wonderful day at work. Sarah, I just want you to know that have gotten over the shock of everything that happened to me and have put them behinde me because i believe it was destined to happen but i didn't pray for such bad things to happen. I wouldn't wish it on anyone.

The issues of my late wife is past and that is why I want to remarry and settle down with a woman who I can grow old with. I've been single since 2009, when she died. I have never felt the touch of woman, let alone of making love with a woman since then.

Thank God you know there's nothing bad in taking care your wife, giving her everything she requests. She normally travel to do shopping in three countries in France, Italy, and Spain. This faithful day, she requested some money for shopping, and I gave it to her. She traveled to Europe and took a direct flight to France. She called me when there and updating me with pics and all she was buying. She did the same thing when she got to Italy. When she got to Spain, she called too, after she has done with her shopping. She decided to get some few things for our son at the Zara store. On her way, they had the accident. i was told the cab driver was over speeding and lost control. I wasn't in the car with her. I was in Canada doing business.

I am happy to hear that your sons are not giving you problem. I am happy to hear that you're proud of them. You know why? It's because you trained them the way they should be. You must be a good mother, Sarah Ellen.

Yes, you're right about the nature of my job. I meet a lot of people, even powerful people through it. I am my own boss, and that suits me.

Sarah, I believe the two men you meet after three years you've been divorced are not the rightful men for you and that was why you didn't end up in marriage. My Sarah, it sounds like our personalities are similar. Communication, love, romantic feelings, caring, understanding and trust are vital in relationship for it to grow and have a solid foundation.

Have a wonderful day at work!

Chrisxoxoxo

MARCO WAS HAVING MORE FUN than usual with this one. Sarah1042 was the thing he needed now that he was between jobs. He closed his laptop on the living room table and walked to the kitchenette on the opposite wall where he poured himself a cup of coffee. His house had two other rooms: a bathroom and his bedroom. Outside, Vinny's chickens clucked in their coop built against the light blue cement block wall that separated their properties.

Vinny lived in his ramshackle house with Cassandra. She was too smart for her own good—always coming up with ways for them to make extra money under the table or fixing them up with her brother's construction company for short-term jobs that needed workers. And she was a stunner, with that tight little body of hers.

Marco would do anything for Vinny—the first friend he made when he arrived in Puerto Rico from technical college in Australia. Both of Marco's parents had died in a car accident in Fiji, and he'd been bereft and reeling.

Marco took his coffee and sat back at the table in the living room. He remembered meeting Vinny in the employment line. He'd hit it off immediately with the short, stocky man. Vinny always helped him, and they'd been through many adventures together; like that time they got caught counting cards in one of the Puerto Rico casinos and Vinny had bribed the security guard, or that time an immigration official had come to their construction job site and Vinny knew where they should hide. He knew he could count on Vinny when the going got tough.

Marco's house was a lot better than many in the town. And he really did work as a building contractor and a security system supplier when he wasn't following through on one of Cassandra's plans. His work was intermittent though, and he could always use the extra money. Life as an immigrant wasn't easy.

As Marco sipped his coffee, he looked into his bedroom. A pile of wires, leftover from his last security system job was piled in the corner. They were a mess, but he'd rather put his energies into Sarah than cleaning them up.

Sarah was so open about her life. That kind of trust online was rare. He bet he could get her to tell him her last name in a few more emails, or maybe after they'd talked on the phone. Then he could check out her finances, her criminal history—even her medical history. He liked the control that gave him. Information was power. It kept the forces of chaos at bay.

Sarah was on the line and he was reeling her in like a big, dumb tuna. He was concerned about the few tugs he'd felt, though—that question she asked about whether he was driving the car when his wife died, or her comment about his "sad story."

As he told Sarah, he even traveled for his job sometimes. He just happened to live someplace other than Boston. The women got suspicious faster if he said he lived in one of the territories or in a foreign country.

Marco grew up in a bilingual household in Fiji. His father spoke Fijian and his mother, who was from Australia, spoke English. Marco spoke English but was never good at writing it. The spelling and grammar rules just never stuck in his head. He was good with numbers, though, and wiring.

With his last message to Sarah, he stopped getting Vinny to edit his writing. It took so long, and he would rather save his money for the other women who weren't hooked yet. Both Vinny and Cassandra spoke Spanish and English, and Vinny was way better at writing English than he was. Marco had picked up a little Spanish, but not enough to target any local women. Besides, that would be too dangerous.

Marco could tell Sarah was really interested. She would overlook a few English mistakes just because he was paying her attention and flattering her. These women were pitiful, so starved for male companionship they'd take it from a stranger on the computer.

He'd given Valerie the boot. Ghosted her. She was all tapped out. But he liked to think it was fun while it lasted. He was giving these women the attention they wanted. It just so happened that he'd take what he wanted, too.

Marco downed the last of his cup and opened his laptop and grinned. Some of his other fishies needed feeding.

YOU HAVE MAIL

From: Sarah1042
To: WillYouBeMine
May 21, 2014

Dear Christopher Edward,

How was your day? Wow, five years is a long time to be by yourself. I'm glad you feel like you can start being with someone again. I don't think people are meant to be alone.

Thank you for what you said about my sons. I'm sure you'd be a good dad to your son if you had him with you.

And yes, it does seem like we have similar thoughts on relationships. It's so refreshing to hear your words about caring and understanding. I think that's so true.

The way you write makes me wonder if English is a second language for you. How long have you been in America?
  Sarah

OUTGOING MAIL
From: WillYouBeMine
To: Sarah1042
May 22, 2014

Hello Beautiful Sarah Ellen,

My day is much better now that I've heard from you. Although I am own boss, I do feel alone sometimes. My next job is not for a week, so I have time on my hand. I wish you were here so I could spend with you, but for now, this emailing will have to do.

English language is a subject I have interest in, is a subject one needs to take time to understand it better because is not difficult to understand if one has much interest in it. That's why it's so easy for me to write, but I am working on my accent. I am mixed race and not a citizen. I am a Fijian. I left Fiji when I was twenty-nine after my both parents died. But I have one uncle who still lives there. He is seventy-five and sick a lot.

I went to Australia where my mother was from to college because there really not much for education in Fiji. I worked some there, enough so that I could have enough money and experience to move to American. Doesn't everyone want to live in America? I am working on getting my citizenship.

I am so happy to have met you, Sarah Ellen, through this sight. I feel so strong about you and I trust you. I trust you enough so that I would give you my personal email address so we can take our conversation off this page. Please, my beautiful Sarah, write to me at chrisedward@msn.com and I will always write back to you.

Have a good sleep and dream of me. I will be dreaming of you.

Chris

Subject: TGIF!

From: Sarah Cartwright <sarahcartwright32@outlook.com>
To: Christopher Kepa <chrisedward@msn.com>
May 23, 2014

Dear Christopher Edward,

What an interesting life you have led. Fiji sounds like such an exotic place! I'd love to go there someday. It's sad that you had to leave it and that your parents died. But lucky for me, you are in America now.

It also sounds like you travel a lot for your job. Do you like to travel? I do. I have good benefits at the university, including several weeks of vacation every year. I would love to have someone to travel with, or someplace to travel to.

I had kind of a hard day at work today, but now, TGIF! Now I have the whole weekend to relax. Where will you be going for your next job? I hope it's somewhere near me in Wisconsin.

Sarah

Subject: Woman of my Dream

From: Christopher Kepa <chrisedward@msn.com>
To: Sarah Cartwright <sarahcartwright32@outlook.com>
May 23, 2014

My Dear Sarah Cartwright,

What a lovely name! I like how it feels on my tongue. Thank you so much for trusting me enough to write to me at my personal email address. I feel very honored by this.

Sad to say my next job will be in Florida, not Wisconsin and next to you. This is to bad, but it is my work nature. I wish it was closer to you so that we could met. I only want to remarry and settle down with the love of my life, the woman of my dream. I love everybody on this earth and i would do everything in my power to support the needs, homeless and the poor people to make them great or be what live a better life.

Honey, I am not a culture type and I don't need my women to be one, so don't be scared but love me for who I am not what I am. Sarah, what do you think of me? Am i fit in to your shoes? Am I the kind of man you woant to settle down or spend the rest of your live with? Would you accept me into your life if I propose to you? Because I am beginning to develop interest in your or let me say have beging to love you more.

Enjoy the rest of your weekend and my regards to your sons.

Chrisxoxoxo

Subject: Too good to be true!
From: Sarah Cartwright <sarahcartwright32@outlook.com>
To: Christopher Kepa <chrisedward@msn.com>
May 24, 2014

Dear Christopher,

I'm so sad you will not be working near Wisconsin. Perhaps I could come to Florida to meet you! I love warm weather, and although it's starting to warm up here, it's never hot enough for me.

You sound like a very caring man, and that appeals to me. You sound almost too good to be true! I'd love to meet you and get to know you better. I imagine that you are so big and strong and could sweep me off my feet. I'd like to see if that is true.

Thank you so much for your question about proposing to me. I've been so lonely, and it's very tempting. But I feel like I should meet you first before I even think about accepting. Would you be willing to pay my airfare to Florida so I could meet you?

You know that I have a good job, but my new car had some weird electrical system malfunctions recently that cost a lot to fix. Otherwise, I could pay for the trip myself. I hate to ask for your help with airfare. I wouldn't except that I'm so looking forward to meeting you. I feel like we could have a serious relationship and a wonderful future together. Please think about it, anyway.

I'm enjoying my Saturday. I will spend it dreaming of you.
Kisses,
Sarah

VINNY WALKED OVER TO THE KITCHEN table where Marco was sitting and handed him a shot of rum. Vinny put the Bacardi bottle in the middle of the scratched wood and sat down opposite Marco and next to Cassandra in one of their mismatched chairs. The darkness of the night hid the dust on the kitchen windowpanes.

"She asked *you* for money?" Vinny's black eyebrows arched above his brown eyes. "That's a first!"

Marco slammed back his drink. "Yeah. I don't know what to do. I don't know how to respond. Do you think she's serious?"

"I don't know." Vinny leaned forward, pouring Marco another. "Maybe she's playing you like you're playing her."

Marco shook his head. "Nah. I just don't get that feeling. She's this lonely secretary in Wisconsin. Don't have nobody. Just wants somebody to love her. I looked up all her intel and she's legit."

Cassandra sat with her elbows on the table, hands flat under her chin. Her long black hair hung down both of her nicely muscled arms, pooling on the table. "Vinny told me you had another one on the line. Aren't you tired of it yet? I'm kinda tired of hearing about them. How many have there been now?" She looked to the ceiling and started counting on her fingers.

Marco narrowed his eyes. "Hey, if it brings money into your house, why should you be tired?"

Cassandra shook her head. "There's always something. Always drama." She paused. "If you think this one's so desperate, then why're you worried when she asks you for a little money?"

"Because it's weird," Marco said. "*I'm* the one who's supposed to ask *her* for money."

The trio exchanged glances, then laughed.

Vinny drank his shot and licked his lips. "I don't know. It just sounds fishy. Maybe you should ask her if she's really serious about seeing you."

"Yeah, and then what?" Marco asked.

"Well, maybe you can tell something from how she answers."

Cassandra chimed in again. "The real question is, do you *want* to meet her?"

Marco felt like someone had punched him in the gut. He sat back and was silent. He thought about the tin box in the nightstand next to his bed—the one with faded pink roses painted on the lid. Inside it was the last photo of him and his parents. His mother smiled out of the Polaroid with her blond hair and blue eyes. He always told the fishies the truth about his childhood and his parents dying later. It was easier to remember that way.

As he thought about his mother in the photo, it dawned on him that Sarah's smile was like his mother's. Sarah was kind like his mother, too—he could tell just from the messages they'd exchanged.

After a moment, he started shaking his head.

"That mean no?" Cassandra asked.

"No, it means I don't believe what I feel."

"Which is?"

"I would like to meet this woman. There's something different about her. Something pure and genuine. Besides, I like her smile."

Cassandra and Vinny locked eyes. Then Vinny looked back at Marco. "Tell me you're not serious," he said.

Marco felt a smile start forming on his lips. "Yeah, I think I am serious. I want to meet this woman."

"Well, that's all you need to know then. Send her the money," Cassandra said.

Subject: Florida
From: Christopher Kepa <chrisedward@msn.com>
To: Sarah Cartwright <sarahcartwright32@outlook.com>
May 25, 2014

My Dearest Sarah,

I am also looking forward so much to seeing you. You should never worry about asking me for help of any kind.

The only problem I see with the idea of you coming to Floirda is that I will be working and won't have much time to attend to you as I should. My plane schedule is already made and cannot be changed so that I could spend more time with you after my work is done there.

If you came to Florida, would you be OK that i have to work every day and not see you much? I worry that you would get bored! And I would want that our first meeting would be perfect. But I so want to meet you! Are you truly serious about this idea? Please don't tease me, for you know my strong feeling for you.

Christopher

MARCO PACED IN FRONT OF THE COUCH in his living room. He hadn't heard from Sarah for two days. Normally, she replied the same day he wrote to her, or at least within twenty-four hours. His pacing took him to the wall calendar in his kitchen. He poked the square that surrounded today's date: May 27. His finger slid over to May 29, where he noted the black X and arrow that marked the days when he would be in Florida. The thick arrow trailed off the page. He flipped the page up and traced the arrow as it continued through the first week of June.

Could something be wrong? Why wasn't she writing back? Memorial Day was the 26th. Maybe it had something to do with that? Vin's warning that Sarah could be playing him passed through his mind. He didn't want to believe it. Surely there was some good left in this hardscrabble, chaotic world—something good, for him?

He could almost see her as she looked in her profile photo, but with the movement of life—her curly blond hair blowing in the wind, her blue eyes crinkling as she laughed. He wanted her to smile his mother's smile for him and him alone.

Marco released the calendar page and strode to the desk where he kept his laptop. He opened his email again to check for Sarah's message. Nothing. He shut the laptop and sighed. He glanced over into the bedroom at the messy pile of leftover wires. His heart felt like that pile.

Then he grabbed his jean jacket off the back of the couch and headed out for a visit to the local bar, El Escorpion. The short walk through his dusty neighborhood took him past other houses much like his own. The sun beat down and the ever-present saltwater breeze ruffled his hair.

He entered the bar and stood still just inside, allowing his eyes to adjust to the dark interior. Black scorpion cutouts covered the walls. A garish red light showed off the long wooden bar. Cassandra and Vinny sat at the far end where he often found them. He made his way over to them and sat next to Vinny.

"Hey, *mis amigos!*" He squeezed Vinny's shoulder.

"Hey, Marco," Cassandra said from Vinny's other side.

"What brings you here in the middle of the afternoon?" Vinny asked.

"Thirsty." Marco caught the bartender's eye and ordered a beer.

Cassandra leaned forward and looked at him closely. "Wait, wait. It couldn't be women trouble, could it?"

Marco cringed, "What makes you think that?"

Cassandra smiled. "Just call it my intuition."

"Well, ya got me," Marco said. "I haven't heard back from Sarah. I'm getting worried something's wrong."

Vinny snorted. "*Pobrecito!*"

"Thanks for the sympathy."

"Sympathy! You're the last one who deserves it. How many women has it been now—twenty, thirty?" Vinny asked.

The bartender set down Marco's beer. Marco took a drink before replying. "Dude, I know what I do to women, but I really feel something for this one. She's special. But I'll be damned if I start begging her. I'll play it cool. The worst thing that could happen is I'll go to work in Florida and not see her. Big deal."

Cassandra flicked her hair over her shoulder. "It looks like someone got past your security system." She looked Marco directly in the eyes. "What if I told you that Sarah isn't real? What if I told you she was just imaginary—that she could disappear in an instant?" Cassandra popped open her hands. "Poof!"

Marco's eyes narrowed. "What the fuck do you mean?"

Even Vinny turned to look at her now. Under his breath he said, "*Aquí hay gato encerrado.*"

"You've been using women for years," Cassandra said.

"Uh-oh," Vinny mumbled. "She's just getting started."

"Damn right." Cassandra looked daggers at them both. "I'm glad you're hurting, Marco. I'm glad you're feeling unsure. *Think* of what you've done to all those women." Her index finger punctuated her point on the bar. "*Think* of how many hearts you've broken. You know that Valerie from Wyoming? It's all over the American news 'cause they got good video. She tried to jump off the state capitol building. A firefighter saved her. You make me sick. I invented Sarah to give you a taste of your own medicine. Maybe get some more money out of you. But after I learned about Valerie—that's why Sarah stopped writing to you." She turned away.

At once, everything made sense to Marco. "You bitch," he said.

"Oh, my dearest Christopher," Cassandra's voice was high, mocking. "I feel so sorry for you with your poor dead wife and your son who hates you—"

"Wait," Vinny's hand tightened around his glass. "You were screwing him over?"

The bartender, on his way to check on their drinks, thought better of it and turned around.

Cassandra grabbed Vinny's arm. "Damn straight. He can't keep doing this. *We* can't keep doing this. It's not right. I want you to promise, Vinny, not to help him anymore."

Vinny barked a laugh. "You're not telling me what to do, woman."

"Okay." Cassandra took her hand off his arm and put both of hers up in surrender. "What if I ask? What if I ask all nice? *Please, Vinny,* stop doing this. Stop making it easy for him to screw over women. What kind of a man would do that anyway? Not one I want to be with."

Vinny glared at her, his voice low and cold. "Why would I want to be with a woman who's messing with my friend?"

Cassandra stood. "Okay, I've had it then. I've had it with the *both* of you." She spat on the floor between their stools. "I'll be gone when you get home."

And she left, slamming the door on her way out.

The two men looked at each other.

Vinny shrugged, "Sorry about that, man. I don't know what got into her."

Marco and Vinny drank another beer and then another, commiserating. Eventually, they graduated to rum. When they emerged from the bar, they swayed home together, arms across each other's shoulders in the dark.

As they passed under a streetlight, Marco swore he heard laughter and saw a blond with his mother's smile flit away into the edge of night.

The House

The woman was drawn in by the house's unchanging nature. She walked her dog on the street in front of it almost every day, as she was about to do now. Although the woman had lived in the neighborhood a dozen years, she only began looking at the house closely during the past few months. It seemed like it was trying too hard to fit in. The one-story structure was gray with white trim and a white front door. Its blinds were always closed; no light ever showed through their slats, even in winter when the dark came early. A driveway on the south side led to the back yard and a gray garage with a white door.

For weeks after she noticed the house, the woman wondered if anyone lived there. Not once did she see anyone mowing the grass. Yet, it never grew past two inches—almost as if the lawn was tended by a robotic mower that came out only at night. No shrubs or flowers adorned the front yard, although some shrubs grew along one side.

In contrast, her own house a few blocks away was two stories and misshapen. The top floor cantilevered out over the bottom in the manner of a rustic brown Swiss Chalet. Her flower garden in the front yard was a mix of flowering weeds, self-sufficient perennials, and some depressed annuals that needed more water than she could remember to give. Her lawn grew in manic spurts that she only thought to control after her neighbors mowed self-satisfied lines of manicured turf on either side.

Recently at the gray house, she'd seen the garage door open a few times, revealing two cars that fit the nondescript theme: one silver, the other black. Someone must be around.

The woman took Cubby's leash off the hook in her mudroom. Her large goldendoodle danced in anticipation of the first of his two daily walks. As she clipped the leash to his collar, she realized it was the sameness of the gray house that bothered her. Nobody could be *that* boring. They must be hiding something behind the ultra-normal façade. She wouldn't be surprised if the house had a hidden basement room or children chained in the attic or bodies buried in the back yard.

She chided herself. Perhaps she'd been watching too many crime shows on TV since she retired. With her husband dying years ago, and both her sons grown and moved away, maybe she had too much time on her hands. Her only relative left in town was her niece Sheila, the librarian. Sheila was busy with her own life, though, and had little time for visits.

Cubby quickly pulled her to the end of her street. They turned left onto the road that veered around the old elementary school and would take them past the house. As the woman and Cubby came even with the yard of that gray house, her heart caught. A tall man with dark hair was walking up the driveway toward the garage. His back was to the street and he held a few white envelopes. She noted his black slacks and white shirt. This concerned her more than if he had been wearing clothing of any other color. *God forbid he wear any blue or green; someone might notice him.*

Cubby wanted to stop and sniff the air trailing the man, but she tugged his leash, not wanting to linger and draw attention. The man kept walking into the open garage. The woman's purposefully nonchalant steps propelled her and Cubby past the house, even though her heart had begun to pound. She and Cubby turned off the pavement and onto the dirt road that led along the end of the school to their favorite trail through a thousand-acre city nature park. She loved the woods; it was her element.

As they walked through the dense forest and her heart slowed, the woman thought. And as she thought, she began to smile.

AT 2 A.M., THE HOUR of deepest sleep, the woman's radio alarm sounded. She clamped her hand down on the clock and got out of bed, groggily changing into black sweatpants and a black hoodie.

Lying alert at the foot of her bed, Cubby followed the woman downstairs to the mudroom off the kitchen. She opened one of the built-in drawers that lined the wall and took out a black neoprene mask she used to protect her face from the winter wind. She considered wearing it but decided it would make her look more suspicious than she already did. She put it back in the drawer and flipped the hood over her graying hair.

"You stay here, Cubby. I'll be back in a little bit."

The dog tilted his head, looking curiously at her as she stepped outside and closed the back door. The late spring air was cool as she walked down the street toward the gray house. The sweetness of lilacs lingered in the night. The woman shoved her chilled hands into her pockets, making a note to wear her black gloves next time.

A waning moon lit her way, bright, but not too bright. She didn't have any trouble finding her way in the dark. All those wilderness camping trips her parents had taken her on as a child made her comfortable moving through the night. When she was very young, she had used a flashlight at first, but the more time she spent away from the comforts of civilization, the more she found she really didn't need artificial light to see her way, especially when the moon was up.

As she neared the gray house, she slowed, scanning the area. All was quiet. A road ran behind the house. Normally busy, it was deserted at this time of night. A stand of trees stood between the road and the garage. Rather than walk up the driveway, she used the road to approach the house from behind. She slipped into the woods and pressed herself to the back of the garage, senses alert. She peeked around the corner toward the back of the house. It was dark and silent. A little rush of adrenaline coursed through her at this adventure, reminding her of when she and her brothers used to play "spy" on the neighbor kids. It had been way too long since she'd felt any sort of excitement or done anything the least bit mischievous.

She slid along the side of the garage to the man door. She always disliked that name, as if only men would ever go into a garage. Well, it was a *woman* door tonight. She turned the handle and the door opened. She smiled and walked inside. The garage smelled like dust and gasoline. A cloying odor she couldn't identify also lingered. She couldn't see a thing, but that didn't bother her. She reached out her hands and walked forward a few steps. They came to rest on smooth metal, which, after more investigating, she discovered was a car trunk.

She turned around and inched toward the wall. Her fingers felt a wooden shelf, and she slowly fondled the things on it, keeping her eyes closed to heighten her sense of touch. A wrench, a pencil, and miscellaneous flotsam. She kept moving and searching. She was looking for a key. Almost everyone she knew had a key to their house hidden somewhere in their garage. *Surely people trying this hard to appear normal would have a key in here.*

She felt around, working her way high and low, careful not to displace a thing. She would not turn on the garage light or use a flashlight. The garage had frosted windows in the door, and she didn't want to get caught. She wouldn't open the car doors, either. That would turn on the dome lights. She noticed that every time she got near one of the cars, the cloying smell got stronger. *Must be an air freshener. Pineapple or something.*

She searched through half of the garage in vain. Stymied, she decided to check if she could hear anything at the house. She made her way out the "woman door," closing it softly behind her. She hesitated a few moments to ensure no one was in the yard. By moonlight, she tried to discern if any security cameras were trained on the back yard. She didn't see any mounted under the eaves or along the roof line. Then she crept the short distance to the back of the house.

The woman stood near the porch. She took off the hood and put her ear to the wall. All was silent until ... *What was that?* A low distant moaning came from within. She pressed her ear harder to the gray siding. A few moments passed and then the moaning came again, like someone hurt. She stepped away, looking up at the back door and the windows, trying to see if anyone was alert to her presence. Nothing. She climbed the few steps to the door, checking to see if it was locked. It was.

Still, the noise had rattled her, and she swallowed hard. After a few more moments to make sure she remained unde-tected, she listened again. It was quiet for a long time, but the moan repeated, more softly. Whoever was hurt, it didn't sound like anyone was coming to help them. An image of a child tied up in the basement came to her. Or maybe it was a woman.

She listened a while longer, then pushed away from the wall, her hands clammy and a chill in her heart. She'd had enough for tonight. Time to go home. She slipped past the garage and back into the trees, grateful for their cover.

WITH CUBBY CURLED ON THE FLOOR at the foot of her bed, the woman tossed and turned as she tried unsuccessfully to get back to sleep. The animal-like groans kept coming back to her. The sounds made her think about those three women who were held captive in Cleveland that had just been rescued. They had been chained to radiators for ten years—having that man's baby and miscarriages without medical aid.

She had to do something to discover the source of those awful sounds.

TWO NIGHTS LATER, AFTER SHE FELT rested and had recovered her bravery, the woman was back in the garage of the gray house, searching through the other half of it like a blind person. She touched a hammer, yard tools, and crusty old paint brushes. Her shin bumped against a wooden stepping stool. She still couldn't find a key.

That same cloying smell hit her whenever she neared the silver car. *Probably covering up the smell of a dead body.*

Since both cars were in the garage, someone must be home. She wouldn't try to enter the house even if she could find the key.

Frustrated, she decided to go to the back of the house and listen again. She pressed her ear to the siding near the porch where she had listened before. She heard nothing at first. She was just about to move when she heard a scuffling and then a low, long moan.

She stepped away and looked for an easy way to enter the house. Since the key wasn't presenting itself, maybe a window would have to do. To her left, past the porch, she saw a screen window about five feet up that could allow entrance, especially if the inner glass was open. Her yoga classes had left her aging body with unusual flexibility. She was sure she could wriggle through the window once she got the screen off, especially if she had something she could stand on.

The dull ache in her shin reminded her of the stepping stool in the garage. *Yes, that would work.* She knew it could be a long wait, but some night when both cars were gone and the window was open, she would use the stool to reach the screen, work it off, and enter the house. With stealth and care she'd investigate the source of the moans and then get out and call the police, if needed. Somehow, she thought the police would be needed.

But how much time did the groaner have? She wished she could call the police now, but what would she tell them? Nothing that sounded sane. She needed specifics.

THE WOMAN WAS MOWING her lawn the next day when one of her neighbors, Wendy, came home from work. Wendy got out of her car and came over. The woman turned off her lawnmower and wiped the sweat from her brow.

"Hi, how's it going?" Wendy asked.

"It's going," the woman said, with friendly flippancy.

Wendy took a closer look at the woman. "Are you sure you're feeling all right? You look a little pale."

Since the woman couldn't very well tell her neighbor she'd been skulking around the neighborhood in the middle of the night, she just said, "I haven't been sleeping well. I think it's the change in the weather."

"I hear ya," Wendy said. "I can't take this heat, myself. I wish we had air conditioning, but it's just not worth it to only use it for a few weeks a year."

"At least we have fans," the woman said. After a moment, she asked, "Say, do you know the people who live in that gray house across from the school?"

Her neighbor scrunched up her face in thought and peered over the woman's shoulder as if she could see the gray house through the trees and houses in between. "No," Wendy said. "I've never seen anyone around that place. I kind of wonder if anyone even lives there. Why do you ask?"

"I wonder if anyone lives there, too," said the woman. "I was just curious, is all. The place looks maintained, but I never see anyone. It's weird." She didn't want to tell Wendy about the man she'd seen, didn't want to let on how closely she'd been watching the house.

"Now you've got *me* curious," Wendy said. "I'll keep an eye out and let you know if I see anybody."

The woman tried to keep her voice casual, "Okay, thanks." Then she changed the subject to the water main shut off that the city was planning for their street tomorrow. They were going to replace the aging pipes.

DURING HER NEXT EARLY MORNING TRIP, a light mist was falling as the woman made her way to the gray house. Disappointment weighed on her as she checked inside the garage and found both cars inside. On her way out the door, she paused to look at the back of the house. The window she hoped to enter was closed. No light came from it or the other windows.

She crept to the other side of the porch near the window this time, hoping to hear the noises better from that location. She pressed her ear to the damp siding and waited, one minute, two, three. Then it came, perhaps a bit louder than before. But this time the moan was punctuated with interruptions—as if it hurt the person to make the sounds—as if they had a broken rib or their arm was twisted behind their back.

Since she knew she wouldn't be breaking in tonight, the woman listened longer than before, repositioning several times, trying to pinpoint the location. She even risked moving to the side of the house which, luckily, was sheltered from the street and the neighbors by bushes.

The groans never grew louder, making her think they were coming from the basement. "AAAAAuugh. Augh. Augh," sifted through the walls into her ears.

"Oh, you poor thing. What have they done to you? I promise, I will help," she whispered into the siding. She imagined the police breaking down the front door and carrying out an emaciated boy in their arms—the child squinting at the bright lights of the squad cars in the night. Television crews would gather and want to interview the woman who alerted police . . . .

The change in the moans spurred a sense of urgency in the woman. Maybe if she came to the house earlier in the evening, the adults would be gone.

The mist grew heavier, threatening to become rain. The woman slipped wraithlike through the backyard trees, on her way home where she planned to investigate how to break into screen windows.

A FEW DAYS LATER, AFTER SHE FELT rested and the weather cleared, the woman awoke to her alarm at 11 p.m. She had gone to bed early so she could get at least a little sleep before her undertaking.

Cubby followed her downstairs from the bedroom. In the closet at the foot of the stairs, the woman dug through a cardboard box that held her tools, bringing out a headlamp that she used inside her tent when she camped, and a pair of needle-nose pliers. In her kitchen, she rummaged through a porcelain plate that held her cell phone and coins, retrieving a couple of paperclips.

She told Cubby to stay, then pulled on her hoodie and went into the night. As she walked down the driveway, Cubby barked as he watched her from a window. It was unusual for him to bark, but she didn't want to waste time going back to quiet him.

When she was about half a block away from the gray house, beams from the headlights of a car came her way. The woman ran off the road and hid behind a tree in someone's front yard. The rough bark snagged on the back of her hoodie as she leaned against it, heart skittering.

After the lights receded, she peered down the street after them, then looked in the other direction toward the house. Everything was clear, so she eased out from behind the tree and continued. Once she reached the house, her quick look in the garage confirmed that both cars were gone. *Yes!* The woman pumped her fist in silent enthusiasm. She felt down low for the stepping stool and crept to the back of the house. As she placed the stool beneath the window, she saw it was open behind the screen. She was so excited she almost didn't bother to check if the groans were still going on in the house.

She pulled off her hood and pressed her ear against the part of the house where she had heard the noises most clearly. After a few minutes, they reached her ears. *I'm coming baby . . . I'm going to help you.*

Back at the window, she climbed the stool. Once up, she put her headlamp strap around her hood. Looking left and right to ensure she was still alone she turned the light on just long enough to find the location of the screen latch. During the brief light, she was also able to see inside the room she'd be entering. She couldn't tell for sure, but it looked like a desk or a dresser was underneath the window.

She stood very still, hoping no one else had seen the flash. An owl in the park hooted its echoey "who-cooks-for-you" call a few times, then was silent. She blinked her eyes to get them used to dark again.

Satisfied, she took out the pliers from her pocket. She inserted the nose into the screen near the latch, making a small hole. Then she pocketed them and took out a paperclip. She straightened a few of its bends, just like the YouTube video on her computer had shown her. She pushed the straightened end through the screen, trying to catch the tip of the latch and push it open. *Damn, I'm not sure I'm aiming it right.*

She switched on her headlamp for a moment and repositioned the paperclip, just a little to the left. She knew her maneuvering was making the hole larger but was sure the homeowners would never notice once she put the screen back in place. And if they did, they'd probably think some animal made the hole, or maybe that it had been there all along.

After a little more futzing, she felt the paperclip bump against the end of the latch. Carefully, she pushed it farther, but it slipped. Cursing quietly, she switched on her light for just a second and repositioned the paperclip. In the dark, she pushed steadily against the tip of the latch. It moved!

She kept pushing until it would go no farther. She knew she had it. Slowly, she removed the paperclip and pocketed it. Then she cautiously pushed the screen inside the room, praying it wouldn't fall and make noise. Just when she felt the screen start to tip, she was able to reach her other hand inside and grab it before it clattered onto the furniture. She stood a few moments, breathing hard, then lowered the screen onto the flat surface below it.

After her breathing slowed, the woman flicked on her light again. Yes, it was a desk. The room looked like an office, with a big clock on the wall and a bookshelf. An open door led to a hallway. She'd be climbing onto a desk strewn with papers; she'd have to be careful not to slip. And she couldn't risk turning her light on again inside the house.

She braced her arms on the window frame and used her yoga strength and flexibility to push her upper body through the window. Silently, she moved the screen off to one side and slid the rest of her body through, squirming like a seal on rocks. She got her knees under her and then sat on the edge of the desk, gradually sliding her feet to the floor. She stood inside the room, getting her bearings.

Somewhere to the right down the hallway, a dim light shone. And somewhere, also from the right, came the groaning. It sounded too near to be coming from the basement. It must be on this floor.

A faint smell of bleach reached her nostrils. She walked through the room silently. Before entering the hallway she paused, listening. Nothing but the groaning. It was coming from the right, near where the light shone, so she turned in that direction.

She passed an empty guest bedroom and then a bathroom on the left side of the hall. That's where the bleach smell was strongest. She lingered outside the bathroom just a moment, looking inside and trying to assess whether anything was amiss, but she couldn't tell. If only she could locate that poor, hurt person, everything would make sense.

The foyer for the back porch and one more closed door were along the right side of the wall between her and the end of the hallway. An open passageway on the left led to the room with the light. *Perhaps it's a kitchen?*

The groans got louder as she progressed, until she stood at the closed door. The sounds emanated from behind it. She couldn't tell if they were from a male or female, young or old. For a moment, she stood, too scared to try the door and find her entry barred after she had come so far. She was so close to the mystery, so close to the discovery . . . .

She tried the door.

It opened.

Inside the room, she immediately noticed a nightlight in a low outlet. On the far side was a mattress on the floor with a dark form on it. She walked closer, making out a misshapen body. Its face was turned toward her, and the groans were coming from its mouth. It was a boy, about ten years old, with dark hair and protruding teeth. His eyelids were closed over bulging eyes. A blanket was bunched up at the foot of the mattress, and his arms and legs were bent at awkward angles.

She looked away for a moment and noticed a wheelchair sitting against the wall on the other end of the room. At once, she realized why the people in this house were trying so hard to look normal on the outside. On the inside, they had this child who wasn't normal.

Just as swiftly, she realized the enormity of what she had done. *I've broken into the house of this helpless boy.*

Of course, he couldn't be alone. Although the cars were gone, there had to be someone home—unless his parents really *were* monsters and had left him here. Maybe she should check the house for them, but everything inside her was urging her to *go.*

She started to turn just as the child opened his eyes. Upon seeing her, his pupils, big and dark already, widened in terror. His mouth opened in an O to emit a howl that was ten times as awful as his groans.

The woman fled, hoping to escape the house through the office. But when she was halfway down the hall, the dark figure of a man came at her.

It was the man she had seen in the driveway those many days ago, but instead of his nondescript clothing, he wore boxer shorts. His hair was tousled, and his face bore a look of sleepy shock. When he saw the woman, he raised his hand, which held something black.

The boy's howls continued, louder than ever.

The woman didn't have time to wish the boy would stop, didn't have time to say anything to the man. She barely had enough time to process that the black thing he held was a gun before her world erupted in a bright flash and a roar.

The last thing she felt was the dull burn as the bullet made a mess of her insides. It tore through her heart and punctured her lung, ricocheting off a rib, lodging somewhere deep inside. Even before her body hit the floor, the woman's soul escaped to the ceiling.

She watched as the man stood over her body, panting. Her lifeless form twitched and writhed mechanically on its back. Her eyes stared, open wide, as if they could see her soul lurking above. Her gray hair snaked around her head on the floor.

The man dropped his gun and raced to the boy. He sat on the edge of the mattress and started to sing, smoothing the boy's hair with his hand. "You are my sunshine, my only sunshine. You make me happy when skies are gray. You'll never know dear, how much I love you. Please don't take my sunshine away."

Eventually, he called 911. The woman watched as the police and paramedics arrived. They didn't even try to revive her. They said she was beyond hope.

In the hallway, a policewoman questioned the man. "You're going to need to come to the station and give a statement, Mr. Roberts," she said.

"I can't leave my son, William." He gestured toward the boy's bedroom. "He's disabled, and my wife is away on a business trip. If I leave, he'll be alone."

The policewoman looked down the hallway at the closed door to the boy's room. "What's the nature of his disability?"

"He's got Pfeiffer syndrome—he can't walk or talk." He drew a shaky hand through his hair. "Christ, he can hardly breathe."

"All right, sir." The woman laid a calming hand on his shoulder. "Let's go into the living room then, and talk. Go get a robe on first, if you'd like."

By this time, more officers had arrived, and one accompanied Mr. Roberts to his bedroom as he put on a green flannel robe and then walked to the living room. The soul-woman followed, floating above.

When the man sat on the couch, he fixed his red-rimmed eyes on the policewoman and told her that something had awakened him. "I figured it was William, like usual, but when I walked past my office, I saw the screen was off the window."

The woman nodded to her colleague, who left in search of the office. "Down the hallway, on the left," she called after him.

"That scared me, so I grabbed the gun I have in my desk. Then William started screaming, and I started running. The woman came at me ... I thought she hurt William. I panicked and ... I shot her." He pressed both hands to the sides of his head. "Why, why, *why* on Earth would she do this?"

The soul-woman didn't like all the angst, all the grief. Like a night fog, she drifted out of the house to the nearby forest where she had always felt at home. She hoped someone would take care of Cubby.

Bog Boy

A Northern Minnesota Romance

A satire of "Bog Girl: A Romance" by Karen Russell

The young birding guide fell hard for her first boyfriend while leading a group through the Sax-Zim Bog. Natalie Heikkala was sixteen, barely old enough to work for the bog nonprofit that catered to birders. These sightseers came from around the world to view rare arctic species stopping over in northern Minnesota on their way to the tundra.

Natalie's eyes were green as the celery that used to grow in fields carved out of drained bogland by Chinese food magnate Jeno Paulucci. Her left eyelid winked in a tic that surfaced whenever nerves ruled her. Natalie made sure her right side was facing Glen, the executive director of the Friends of the Sax-Zim Bog during her interview about the guiding job.

How did Natalie persuade Glen to hire her? She laid claim to many qualities, only some unfounded: maturity, a keen eye and ear for birds, and a love of walking trails. Glen took her outside the visitor center to test her on the few straggling songsters left on a September evening. Judging from his grimace, Natalie got a few wrong. Then she pointed to her bedroom window, a quarter mile away on the edge of the gravel road that ran through the bog, where undrained bog water still sparkled in the ditch between the tamaracks. The intimation was clear—what the thin, strange girl lacked in bird identification she made up for in proximity to the work site. Applicants weren't exactly pounding down Glen's door for this job in the middle of nowhere.

The vast peatlands of northern Minnesota cover more than ten percent of the state. Unlike the clearing of the prairies and white pine forests, efforts to drain and develop the bogs were mostly failures, although unnaturally straight ditches testify to this toil. The bottom of a peatland is a breathless place—cold, acidic, anaerobic—with no oxygen to decompose branches or the small, still faces of the weasels interred there. Sphagnum mosses wrap around the fur, wood, and skin, casting their spell of chemical protection, preserving them whole. Growth is impossible, and Death cannot complete his spare work.

Minnesota's peatlands formed over five thousand years ago when the climate cooled and rain increased. The state contains more peatlands than any other in the U.S., except its Alaskan stepsister. Bogs hold twenty percent of the planet's carbon. Now, as the climate warms, they are beginning to release their ancient stores, accelerating the problem.

Although in the U.K. and northern Europe the smoky glow of peat still heats many houses, the trend never caught on in Minnesota. Not even in Natalie's hometown of Meadowlands, which was surrounded by the stuff.

In Europe, bogs were portals to distant worlds, wilder realms. Gods traveled the bogs. In America, peatlands were just an inconvenience to be drained or avoided. Even the Ojibwe left them alone. Maybe that's why birds loved Sax-Zim. It was a place where people were not. The owls could hunt voles, mice, and moles in peaceful content.

On the morning in the cusp of spring when Natalie found the Bog Boy, she was leading a group of six down Gray Jay

Way, a trail that ran from the visitor center to the murky intersection of two drainage ditches. Over the winter, she'd gained enough experience so that the birders no longer complained about her to Glen. Although prime spring birding season lay a few weeks off, she'd managed to nab sightings of a yellow-rumped warbler and a rare Virginia rail for this group. Natalie patiently answered the birders' questions about each, reminding herself she had a higher purpose: she was saving to buy an ATV. Once she had it, she could join the caravans roaming the primitive forest roads, partying in parking lots and rustic campsites, find a little freedom from her father. She might even meet a boy—not one from her school. They were more like brothers. She wanted a boyfriend.

Natalie was far too shy to have an eye-level crush on anyone at school, anyway. Not Shane, not Erik, not Greyson, not Hal. She had a crush, taboo and distressing, on her uncle Charlie's toned calf muscles when he wore shorts. She had a crush on the anonymous muscled backs of shower gel models on TV.

The previous day, a hard rain fell, flooding cities and towns downstream. People in Duluth, the largest city nearby, suffered road washouts and flooded basements as the water rushed down the hillside and into Lake Superior's vastness. In Meadowlands, the bog soaked it all up, like a giant sponge.

Natalie had just settled the birders on the wooden viewing platform at the trail's end, orienting them to the species owning the songs when she looked at the side of the bog ditch and screamed. A hand stuck out of the near side. As she understood what she saw, her first words to the Bog Boy rose in pitch and intensity, drowning out the birds: "Ohmygaaaawwwwwwd!"

Here was a secret, flagging her down. A secret the murk had kept for two thousand years and been unable to keep a moment longer. The bog confessed him to her.

Natalie ran to the hand. Kneeling, she was tearing away clods of peat when the birders arrived. Already she had dug out the bog boy's head. He was whole, all his limbs intact, cradled in peat and curled like a sleeping chipmunk. His thick, lustrous hair fanned over the ground, either the wild red-orange of a Viking or dyed by bog acids. Perhaps both. Moving clouds caused his colors to morph: now they were a tawny bronze, now a mineral blue. His face was young with high cheekbones and a delicate beard covering the line of his jaw like a spider web.

Gently holding his head, Natalie lost all feeling in her legs. A light rain began to fall, but she would not leave her boy. The birders stared. Ordinarily, their attention prickled Natalie like a crown of thorns, making her self-conscious, twitching her eye. Today, she didn't give a damn about these tourists with their binoculars and Eddie Bauer clothing. Who had ever seen a face so peaceful, so handsome?

One birder broke the silence. "Is he alive?"

"Of course he's not!" said another.

"Somebody check his pulse!"

A man knelt next to Natalie. Sensing her possessiveness, he asked, "Is it okay?"

Natalie nodded and the man peeled back the coarse tan cloth from the boy's wrist. He slowly shook his head and turned to the others. "I think this guy's been dead for a long time."

Natalie didn't know what to do except that she couldn't leave. She whispered to the man who still knelt beside her. "Could you go get Glen, tell him what's happened?"

"All right then. I'll take the others back, too."

While she waited, the bog boy drew her in. If you saw him from one angle only, you would assume he was a cherished son, laid to rest by hands that loved him. But if you looked at him from another, something about his neck was off. Had it been broken? From a *National Geographic* magazine in her attic, Natalie had read about people killed thousands of years ago in the bogs across the sea, sacrificed to appease ancient angry gods or convicted of powerful crimes, left to mummify silently in the murk.

His lips formed a soft smile, calling forth a maternal drive in Natalie to protect. She could hear Glen puffing down the trail, feet trampling the tall sedges. He stopped a few feet away, bent over with hands on his thighs, wheezing. "Natalie, what the hell?"

She looked up at Glen, eyes narrowed.

"Is he really dead?"

Natalie nodded, drawing the boy closer.

"Oh shit. I'm going to have to call the sheriff." He stood and took his phone from his back pocket, punched the sheriff's number on speed dial.

As Glen spoke, he kept calling the boy "the body," which baffled Natalie—the term seemed so remote from the deep and flowing dream life beyond the boy's smile. "There's more to you than what Glen sees," she reassured him in a whisper. "I'm sorry about what happened to you. I'll keep you safe."

After this secret conversation, Natalie fell rapidly in love. She was lucky to meet her boyfriend in such a remote place. When these bodies are found in Ireland or in the humid Florida bogs sprinkled between Disney World and Cape Canaveral, things proceed differently. The area is cordoned off. Teams of experts arrive to excavate the site. The bog people are carefully removed to laboratories, museums, where gloveless hands never touch them.

Natalie touched his hair, touched his crooked neck. The sheriff and two deputies arrived. They conferred above Natalie, their brown boots squeezing mud around the bog cottongrass. Once they determined the boy was not a recent murder victim and that no laws had been broken, the lawmen relaxed. The sheriff asked Natalie a single question: "You're going to keep him, then?"

ARNE HEIKKALA WAS SITTING in his La-Z-Boy recliner watching the Vikings play the Packers on TV. The Vikes were losing. The football stadium's roar had just subsided when he glanced at Natalie and the Bog Boy settled on the couch across the room. Their long silences unnerved him; surely, they weren't getting into trouble, ten feet away? He had to watch this girl. She was headstrong, sneaky—like the time she got that job as a bird guide. He would have never given her permission for that but found out once it was too late. As a lesson, he made her give him half of what she earned. If she was old enough to get a job, she was old enough to start paying for the food she ate and the roof over her head.

At least her boyfriend didn't eat much. Arne snorted. It was about time Nat started showing some interest in the opposite sex. The Heikkala family aunts and uncles had started asking if she was a lesbian. As if!

Sister Viola had seen a picture of the Bog Boy in the *Meadowlands Chronicle*. She phoned Arne, saying, "Sixteen is such a hard age. We were all sixteen once. We all survived."

Brother Charlie worried about the age difference. "Natalie is only *sixteen*. Her boyfriend is at least two thousand! You gotta warn them about the consequences."

A professor had also read the story of the Bog Boy's discovery. He'd driven all the way from Minneapolis to find them. He wanted the boy for the university museum. Offered half of Arne's annual salary at the paper mill.

In the end, what had happened? A strange feeling had muzzled Arne. How could he sell his girl's boy to this stranger? How could he take this Viking, or whatever he was, away from this land? Arne told the prof that the Bog Boy was their houseguest and would be living with them until social services could locate his next of kin. At this, all the veins in the professor's neck stood out like angry purple worms. His tone sank into petulant defeat. "Mark my words, you people do not have the knowledge to properly care for him," he said. "He'll fall apart on you."

The Bog Boy, propped up next to the ironing board, listened to them argue with an implacable smile. The university man left empty-handed, and for a night and a day, Arne was a hero to his daughter.

"So, he's just freeloading then? Living off your coin?" Viola asked.

"Oh yeah, the dude's shameless about it," Arne said.

How could he explain to his sister what he could barely admit to himself? His girl was in love. It was a monstrous, misdirected love; nevertheless, it commanded respect.

Charlie pushed his brand of worry harder. "The Bog Boy is a bad influence on Nat. All day he lazes around the house. He cannot *stay* with you! You should put him back in the bog. You could do it tonight. Who's going to miss him?"

"I can't put him back in the bog. It would be . . ."

He didn't know how to say it. Yes, it was wrong but at least he knew where his daughter was. She was *his* daughter and he would decide what was best, not his nosey family. When he was in high school and got his girl pregnant, they had made it quite clear he was sacrificing his future. When she was five months gone, Arne and his girlfriend ran off. He'd returned to the boglands alone with a bug-eyed toddler. His family wanted him to put Nat up for adoption.

"I'm afraid," he confessed to Charlie. "If I put him out of the house, she'll leave with him."

THE FIRST TWO WEEKS, the Bog Boy slept on the sofa in their house with the Tyvek vapor barrier siding. Their place was perpetually under construction. A mobile home where they used to live slumped in the back yard. The television light flickered gently over the boy. Then, on a rainy Monday night, without warning or apology, Arne's skinny but sturdy Natalie picked up the Bog Boy. She cradled him like a child, his dull bronze feet dangling in the air like levitating mushrooms.

Arne, doing a jigsaw puzzle of a Canadian Mountie in the kitchen, looked up in time to see them disappearing down the hall. He felt a purple welt rising in his mind. Underneath the shock, other feelings began to flow, among them a disturbed pride. Because hadn't she looked *exactly* like her mother? Natalie didn't ask for her father's permission. She did not lie about what she was doing, or hide it, or explain it. She simply rose with the Bog Boy in her arms, nuzzling his blue neck. The door shut, and she was gone from sight. Another milestone: he heard the click of the lock.

What was he supposed to do now? Go over there and pound on the door? Arne half-rose. He stayed crouching for several moments, then sat to think, drumming his hand over shifting puzzle pieces.

In the morning, he watched the nimble movements of Natalie's hands as she worked with the coffeepot. So, she was a coffee drinker now. News to him. She kissed her father's forehead as she left for work, but she was whistling to herself, oblivious to her father's sadness and anger, completely self-enclosed in her new happiness.

Before the front door could slam, Arne yelled, "Natalie!" She stopped and turned to look at him, her arm catching the door. "New rule," he said. "Everyone has to wear clothes. And no more locked doors."

ONE WARM SATURDAY, Natalie took the Greyhound four hours to the Science Museum of Minnesota. Twelve bog bodies were on display, part of a traveling exhibition called "Kings of the Iron Age." The Bog Boy had met her family—the least she could do was return the favor. Natalie sneaked into a tour in progress, following a docent from sepulcher to sepulcher. The kings of the Iron Age lay like dried deer hide under glass. One man was naked except for a fox-fur armband. Another was a giant. Another had two sets of thumbs.

Natalie learned that the bogs of the islands in the cold Atlantic were particularly acidic. Pickled bodies from the Iron Age had emerged from these deep vats. Their curled bodies often doubled as the crumpled maps of murders. They might have been human sacrifices, the docent said, left in the bog water for the harvest god. Kings, failed king candidates, queens, scapegoats, victims—they might have been any of these things.

What had her Bog Boy been? She mused that he was a Norse explorer—like one of the Vikings who carved the rune stone in Alexandria, only a few days' travel by foot. Perhaps, like the members of that party, he met with some mishap and his companions buried him in the bog rather than haul him for burial in soil that could be many miles away.

"From the contents of his stomach, we can surmise he last dined on oat gruel . . ."

"From the forensic analyses, we can surmise she was killed by an arrow . . ."

"From the ornaments on this belt buckle, we can surmise these were a wealthy people . . ."

What? No more than this could be surmised?

The docent pointed out the dots and stripes on the pot sherds—charcoal smudges that might be stars or animals. Evidence, she said, of "a robust culture." Natalie took notes:

THEY HAD TIME TO KILL. THEY LIKED ART, TOO.

Back on the bus, she could admit her relief: none of the other bog bodies stirred any feeling in her. She loved one specific person. She could see things about the Bog Boy to which this batty docent would be totally blind. For example, the secret depths his smile concealed. How badly misunderstood he had been by his own people. He was an alien from a planet that nobody alive could visit—the planet Earth, the first century A.D. Although he was heavy in her arms, he felt boneless, rubbery, indestructible.

According to the experts, a bog body should begin to decompose rapidly when exposed to air. Curiously, her Bog Boy had not. She told no one her theory but polished it inside her mind like an agate: it was her love that protected him.

BY AUGUST, THEIR RAPPORT had deepened. They didn't need to say a word to perfectly understand each other. Natalie was discovering that falling in love with the Bog Boy was wonderful—it was permission to ignore everything else. When school began in September, she made a sling and brought him with her. He stood, propped like a broomstick against the rows of lockers, waiting for her during Biology and Music II, as cool and impassive as the most popular boy the world has ever known.

Nobody in the school administration objected to the presence of the Bog Boy. They had all read about him in the newspaper. Here was a celebrity in their school. Soon he was permitted to audit all of Natalie's classes, smiling patiently at the flustered teachers.

One afternoon, the vice-principal called the Bog Boy into his office and presented him with a red-and-gold badge to wear in the halls: VISITING STUDENT.

"I don't think that's really accurate, sir," Natalie said.

"Oh no?"

"His eyes are shut, so I don't think he can really, uh, study."

"Well!" The vice-principal clapped his hands. He had a school to run, quotas to fulfill. "We will be studying *him*, then. He will give us all an exciting new perspective on our modern life and times—oh my! Oh gosh." The Bog Boy had slumped into his aloe planter.

Natalie put the badge on the boy's cotton T-shirt, a loaner from her father. Natalie—who rarely gave a thought about her own clothing—enjoyed dressing the Bog Boy for school in the morning. She raided her father's closet, resurrecting worn plaid shirts. The eleventh-grade girls organized a clothing drive for the Bog Boy, collecting thrift-store donations of dress shirts, jeans, Carhartt jackets, and trendy boots.

Rumors sprawled. Word got around that the Bog Boy was actually a prince. A prince or possibly a knight. Within a week, he was eating at the popular girls' table. They'd kidnapped him from where Natalie had positioned him on a bench, propped between two book bags, and taken him to lunch. Already they had restyled his hair into a man bun.

"You stole my boyfriend," Natalie said, her eye twitching.

"Something *awful* must have happened to him," Cindy said reverently.

"So bad," Tiffany echoed.

"He doesn't like to talk about it," Stacie said, looping a protective arm around the Bog Boy.

The girls had matching lunches: lettuce salads, diet candy bars, diet shakes. They were all jealous about how little he ate.

How had Natalie not foreseen this turn of events? The Bog Boy was a wounded mysterious redhead. Best of all, he could never contradict any rumor the living girls distributed about him.

"He was too handsome to live!" Stacie gasped. "They killed him 'cause he was too good-looking."

"I don't think it happened quite like that." Natalie covered her left eye with her hand.

The popular girls adjusted their leggings, annoyed. "No?"

Natalie was dimly aware that the other tables were listening in, but the density of the attention in no way affected her. "I am his, and he is mine," she announced, dropping her hand from her eye, now still. "I have dedicated my life to learning everything about him."

A sighing spasm of envy moved down the popular girls' table. They wished someone would be as interested in them, some boy. Nobody mocked Natalie Heikkala. They were all starving to be loved like this. They moved aside so she could sit next to the Bog Boy. The girls watched the couple avidly. Natalie ate her grilled cheese and waffle fries, her green irises burning. Between bites, her left hand rose to touch the Bog Boy's red man bun, plucking off the band like the pull-chain of a lamp.

ARNE FELT HIS GIRL SLIPPING AWAY, their past erasing. It had been just the two of them against the world when he'd come back to Meadowlands. Did she remember the care with which he'd cut the tiny moons of her fingernails? The lullabies he sang to soothe her to sleep? His daughter had matured into amnesia about her earliest years.

"There's so much about yourself that you do not remember," Arne accused her after dinner one night. Natalie, writing a paper about igneous rocks at the kitchen table, did not look up. "When you were small, you used to be scared of the vacuum cleaner." Agony laced Arne's voice. "I used to have to get Uncle Charlie to take you on a walk just so I could clean the carpet. You used so much glue on your art projects that your teachers—"

"What's with these dumb stories, Dad?"

"Oh, you find them dumb, do you? The stories about how I had to raise you alone, without any help from your no-good ma?"

"You're just trying to *embarrass* me in front of him!"

The Bog Boy smiled at them from his chair at the table. His leather jacket was cropped short, a donation from Stacie. Bugs spun in his water glass, mosquitoes and dragonflies were always diving into the Bog Boy's food and drink, as if in solidarity.

Natalie drew herself up, stood in front of her father. "You don't want me to grow up."

"What? Of course I do!"

Natalie was ready with her rebuttal: "Then what's with all the rules? I feel like I'm choking."

"You're so young, you can't know ..." Arne's body seemed to cave in on itself then, becoming smaller and smaller, so that even Natalie, fortressed behind the wall of her love, noticed.

"Dad, what's wrong?"

"It's changing all the time," he muttered ominously. "Just please, wait, Nat. Don't ... *settle*." He pictured his daughter sinking up to her neck in black bog water. He had to come out and say it. "I don't want you to throw your *life* away on some Bog Boy!" He uncrumpled a bit, stood with fists clenched.

Natalie took one of his fists into her hands, stroked it. "Oh Dad. Don't you know I'm not going anywhere?"

THE BOG BOY FLOATED, thin as a reed, on the mattress. He smiled at Natalie, or beyond her, with his desiccated calm. Downstairs, Arne was making breakfast, the buttery smells threading through Natalie's nose like a piercing, tugging her toward them. But when her father called for her, she was barely in the room. She was digging and digging into the peat-moss bog again, smoothing the Bog Boy's blue cheeks with both hands, spading down into the realm he came from.

"Nat! The bus is coming!" It should have taken her twenty seconds to put on pants. Arne wondered what she was doing in there. Probably buying cologne for the Bog Boy with her new credit card.

"Coming!" Natalie said.

She was always learning new things about her boyfriend. The longer she looked at him, the more she saw. His face grew silty with personality. Although he was young when he disappeared into the bog, his face was plowed with tiny wrinkles. Some dream or mood had recurred often enough to hammer lines across his brow. Here were the ridges and gullies his mental wonders had worked into his skin.

Natalie studied the root lines on his cheeks. His brain is in there, the university man had said. His brain is intact, preserved by the bog acids. Natalie spent hours doing this forensic palmistry, trying to read his mind.

"WILL YOU HAVE A TALK WITH HER?" Arne begged Charlie. "Something is going really, really wrong!"

"First love, first love," Charlie muttered, scratching his long nose. "Who are we to intervene, eh? It will die of natural causes."

"Natural causes!"

Arne was thinking about the Bog Boy's neck. It must have been twisted by strong hands, quick and purposeful. You could not survive your death, could you?

IN MID-OCTOBER, A STRETCH limousine pulled up on the gravel road to the house to take Natalie and the Bog Boy to the annual school dance. A techno-pop song called "Blurred Lines" filled the back seat, where half a dozen teenagers sat in churchlike silence. The Bog Boy's reticence was contagious. Passing police car lights sparkled through the tinted windows, causing everyone to jump, with one exception: Natalie Heikkala's date, the glamorous foreigner, or native—nobody was sure how to regard him.

Since acquiring a far older boyfriend, Natalie had begun speaking to her classmates in the voice of an experienced woman who merely tolerates children. "Tiffany," she said, clearing her throat, "would you mind exhaling a little closer to the window? Your vaping is blowing on us."

Two girls started debating whether or not a friend in the limo should lose her virginity in a Hummer that evening. What was the interior of the SUV like? This was a very important question. The girl's boyfriend was a twenty-six-year-old mine worker from the Iron Range. Prior to the Bog Boy's arrival on the scene, everyone had found the boyfriend's age impressive. The miner boyfriend had to work and could not accompany the girl to the school dance, so she had to take poor Artie, her sophomore cousin, who sat looking near fatally compressed by his green cummerbund. The twenty-six-year-old would be waiting for her in his Hummer, post-festivities. Should she deflower him?

"Wait. Uh. I think he's deflowering you, right? Or maybe you're deflowering each other? Who's got the flower?"

"Just do it and lie about it." Cindy shrugged. "That's what I did."

"My advice," Natalie said in the unfamiliar voice, "is to wait. Wait until you find the person with whom you want to spend all your earthly time." The Bog Boy leaned against her shoulder, aloof in his checkered dress shirt and khakis. "Or until that person finds you. If that's this guy, well, kudos. But, if not, wait. You will meet your soulmate. And you will want to give that person every molecule of your life."

The attempted conversion of the high-school gym into an Arabian-themed wonderland had not been a success. Natalie and the Bog Boy stood under a palm tree that looked like an enormous toilet brush made of cellophane and cardboard tubes. Two boys from the limo came up and asked Natalie to dance, but she explained that her boyfriend hated to be left alone. All were sulkily respectful of his claim on her.

The after-party was held in an old barn on the western outskirts of town, where everything else was shut or abandoned; despite the popularity of the bog with birders, the small population of Meadowlands had been declining to an even smaller one for three decades. The music sounded like fists beating on the wall. The floor was so sticky that Natalie had to lift the Bog Boy, looping the trailing legs of his pants around one arm. Natalie had never attended an after-party before. Or a party, for that matter. She surveyed her former tormentors, the seniors, with their farm-bland faces and their red plastic cups. Some were single, some had boyfriends, some were virgins, some were not, but not one of them, Natalie felt very certain, knew the first thing about love.

Artie the sophomore came over, his date nowhere to be seen. He was breathless in the cummerbund, in visible danger of puking up Boone's Farm wine. He rolled a bloodshot eye in Natalie's direction, smiling wistfully.

"So," he began, "I'm just wondering. Do you guys—"

Natalie preempted the question: "A lady never tells." It was a phrase she'd read once in an ancient women's magazine while waiting to see the dentist. In fact, her father needn't have lost so much sleep to this particular fear. At night, Natalie lay beside the Bog Boy, barely touching him. A steady, happy calm radiated from him, which filled her with a parallel euphoria. And that was enough.

Natalie carried the Bog Boy onto the dance floor, his hair flowing over her shoulder. Even Artie, minutes from unconsciousness, could see exactly who the older girl believed herself to be in this story: Natalie the Rescuer.

"Oh damn! Wise up! Boys don't need girls to rescue them!" Artie's lonely laugh died a terrible death, like a small bird impaled on a thorn by a shrike.

AT 3 A.M., THE LIGHTS were still on. *Uh-oh*, Natalie thought. *Dad got into the gin again.*

Drinking made his silences bubble volubly. She almost got the hiccups herself, listening to his silences. *Oh, God.* She knew there was so much pain inside of him, so much he wanted to share with her but couldn't. Natalie and the Bog Boy tried to tiptoe past him to her room, but her father sprang up like a jack-in-the-box.

"Nat?" He looked smaller than usual in the dark. His voice was tremulous, and his blinking eyes reminded her of her own tic, that undead vestige of her early years. His feet were bare, and he rose onto his long toes to grip Natalie's arm, swaying a little. "Where are you coming from?"

"Nowhere. The dance. It was fun."

"Where are you going?"

"Dad, where do you think? To bed."

Arne held her a moment longer, looking past the lump of the Bog Boy in her arms and into her eyes. "You look real pretty."

Natalie shook herself free. "Don't be creepy Dad. You get so gross when you're drunk."

He called after her, "I hope you had a good time!"

BY EARLY WINTER, the Bog Boy's stillness had begun to provoke a restlessness in Natalie, a squeezed and throbbing feeling. She was failing three subjects. Her father had threatened to send her to live with Aunt Viola until she "straightened out." She didn't care. Waiting for the bus in the freezing rain, she no longer dreamed of owning an ATV. She knew what she would do with her money from guiding: run away with the Bog Boy.

She'd flunk out of school and take him with her to Duluth, or better yet, St. Paul. He'd be homesick at first, maybe, but they'd go on trips to urban parks. It was the burr of peace, the burr of happiness, goading her onto new movement. Oh, she was frightened, too.

With a strange joy, she imagined the narrow life they would lead. No children, no sex, no messy nights vomiting outside bars, no unintended pregnancies, no fights in the street, no betrayals, no surprises, no promises, no broken promises.

Was the Bog Boy a cosigner to this fantasy? Natalie had every reason to believe so. When she described her plans to him, the smile never left his face. Was their love one-sided, as the concerned and unimaginative adults in her life kept insisting? No—but the proof of this surprised no one more terribly than Natalie.

One night in mid-December, lying in bed, she felt a cobwebby softness on her left cheek. It was his eyelashes, flicking over her. They glowed radish red in the moonlight. Natalie swatted at her face, her own eyes never opening. Still sunk in her dreaming, she moaned and rolled over.

Natalie.

Natalie.

The Bog Boy sat up.

With fluttering effort, the muscles of his lightly bearded blue jaw opened his mouth in a yawn. One eye opened. It studied itself in the dresser mirror for a long instant, then turned calmly back to Natalie. Very slowly, his left arm unhinged itself and dropped to the plaid bedspread. The fingers curled around the blanket's edge and drew it down. A blush of primal satisfaction colored the Bog Boy's cheeks as the fabric moved. He tugged more forcefully, revealing Natalie curled on her side in her white tank top and undies. Groaning in her sleep, she jerked the covers back up.

"Natalie," he said aloud.

Now Natalie was awake—irreversibly awake. She blinked up at his face, which was staring down at her. When they locked eyes, his frozen smile widened.

"Dad!" she couldn't help screaming. "Help!"

The Bog Boy, imitating her, began to yell. And Natalie could see, radiating from his gaze, the same blind tenderness that she had directed at him. Now she was its object. Something truly terrifying had happened: he loved her back.

For months, Natalie had been decoding the Bog Boy's silences. She'd tried to translate his dreams, his fears, his innermost thoughts. But his real voice was nothing like the voice she'd imagined for him—a cross between Richard Gere and Justin Timberlake. Its loud ululations hailed over her.

Somewhere outside, a dog began to bark. The language he spoke was no longer spoken anywhere on Earth.

She stumbled up, tugging on her robe. The Bog Boy stood, too. The past, with its monstrous depth and span, reached toward her, demanding an understanding that she simply could not give. Her mind was too young and too narrow to withstand the onrush of his life. An invisible forest was in the bedroom with them, the scent of trees multiplying. Some mental earthquake inside the Bog Boy was casting up a world, green and unknown to her, or to anyone living. His gaze drove inward, carrying Natalie with it. For an instant, she thought she glimpsed his parents. His brothers, his sisters, a nation of people. Their cheeks now beginning to brighten, every one of them alive again inside his village. Pines rippling seaward. Great wooden ships, their bows covered with gods, horned and faceless, plied the great ocean. Natalie was buried in water, in liquid images of him; she had to push through so many strata of his memories to reach the surface of his mind. Most of what she saw she shrank away from. Her mind felt like a burned tongue, numbly touching his reality.

"Wh-wh-who are you?"

Heartbreak is the universal diagnosis for the pain that accompanies the end of love. But this was an unusual breakup, in that Natalie's mind shattered first. The fantasy that had protected her began to fall away. Piece after piece of it clattered from her chest, an armor rusting off her. "What are you?" Natalie whispered.

The Bog Boy lurched toward her, his arms open. First, he moved like a hopping chick, with an unexpected buoyancy. Then he seemed to remember how to step, heel to toe. He came for her like an astronaut, bounding on the gray carpet. The only English word he knew how to say was her name.

Almost weightlessly, he reached for her. For wasn't he equally terrified? There was no sanctuary other than this girl, who had gripped him with her thin, freckled arms, bellying him out of the peat bog and into time.

Natalie hid behind the dresser.

His reaching fingers found her hand, threaded through her fingers.

She screamed again, even as she squeezed his hand back.

His words rushed together, a thawing waterfall, moving intricately between octaves; still the only word Natalie understood was her name. Perhaps nothing she had said to him in their time as a couple had been comprehended. Natalie worked the levers in her brain, desperately trying to find the words that would release her.

"What's going on?" her father's voice called.

Natalie was frozen in the Bog Boy's grip, unable even to call out. But a moment later, she saw the light from the hall flood underneath her door. The knob turned. Arne stood in the doorway in his blue-striped pajamas. With panoramic comprehension, he took in what had happened. He knew, too, what must now be done. If he could have freed these two from the embrace himself, he would have done so; but now he understood the challenge. The girl would have to make her own way out. "Take him home, Nat. Make sure he gets home safely."

Natalie, her eyes round with panic, only nodded.

Arne went to the Bog Boy, helping him into a sweater. "Put a hat on. And pants."

Her father shepherded them downstairs and onto the porch, switching on every yellow bulb as they moved through the house. It was the warmest winter on record so far, rain falling instead of snow, the drops disappearing into the rotted wood. Natalie carried the Bog Boy to the edge of the light before she understood that her father was not coming with them.

"Let him down gently, Natalie!" her father called.

Well, he could do this for her, at least: he held a lantern steady across the rainy lawn, creating a gangplank of light that reached almost to the tamaracks. He watched them moving toward the inky water. The Bog Boy was howling in his foreign tongue and at this distance, Arne felt he could almost understand it.

Oh, he hoped their breakup would stick. He had left Natalie's mother, then briefly moved back in with her. It had taken years before their affair was truly over. You had to really cultivate an ending. To get it to last, you had to kneel and tend to the burial ground, continuously firming your resolution.

This was a bad breakup. A quarter mile from the house, under a bright moon, Natalie and the Bog Boy were rolling in the mud, each screaming in a different language. Their yells twined together, their hands, reaching for each other; it was during this undoing that they were, at last, truly united as a couple.

Natalie's flashlight rolled with them, plucking amphibious red and yellow eyes out of the reeds. "It's over. It's over. It's over," she kept babbling optimistically, out of her mind with fear. The Bog Boy's throat was vibrating against her skin. She could feel the echo of her own terror and sorrow, and again her mind felt overrun by the lapping waves of time.

He clutched at the neck of her tank top, his body covered in dark mud and cracked stems of cottongrass, blue lichen. At last she felt his grip on her loosen. His eyes, opaquely glinting in the moonlight, liquid and far larger than anyone could have guessed before unlidded, regarded her with what she imagined was hard surprise and disappointment. She was not who he'd expected to find when he opened his eyes, either.

Now neither teenager needed to tell the other that it was over. It simply was. Without another sound, the Bog Boy let go of Natalie and slipped backward into the bog water. Did he sink? It looked almost as if the water rose to cover him. His cranberry hair waved away from his scalp. As she watched, his body began to break up.

Straightening from where she was kneeling on the edge of mud, she brushed peat from her pants. Her arms tingled where his grip had suddenly relaxed. The clear rain began to drench her clothing. The bog was still bubbling, pieces of him sinking into the black peat, when she turned on her heel and ran.

"Dad! Dad!" Natalie came racing out of the dark, pumping her knees as she ran for the light, for her home at the edge of the boglands. "Who was that?"

For the next few days, she would be quaky with relief; she'd felt certain, watching him sink away, that she would never see the Bog Boy again in this life.

But here she was mistaken. In the weeks to come, Natalie would find herself alone with his memory, struggling to pay attention to her droning contemporaries in the cramped classroom. How often would she retrace her steps, wandering right back to the lip of the bog, peering in? Each dusk, with primitive eloquence, airborne insects continued to speak the million syllables of his name.

The Shower Singer

. . . When those who enjoy a hot bath inhale the air of the bath, so that the heat of the air enters their spirits and makes them hot, they are found to experience joy. It often happens that they start singing, as singing has its origin in gladness.

—Ibn Khaldun, from "Muqaddimah," 1377 AD

Sam sat at the chipped yellow Formica table in his kitchen, slurping milk from his cereal bowl. The cereal box next to him proclaimed that Honey Sunshine was a healthier, organic alternative to Captain Crunch. He wasn't so sure.

He ate a spoonful. His teeth ground through the rough squares. Sam mulled his situation. He hadn't written a song in a couple of months. No melodies drifted into his head. Not even tuneless lyrics. He wasn't inspired.

Being songless was boring. Eating this cereal was boring. It was like chewing thirty-grit sandpaper with a bunch of sugar sprinkled on top. Lord knows his mouth could use a clean start, but this wasn't the way he wanted to get it.

Maybe it had something to do with Selene. They had broken up six months ago after she got frustrated by his schedule. At first, after their breakup, he was at least able to write morose songs. Now nothing—as if the longer he was away from her, the more his creativity diminished.

When they met, he was the noon entertainment at an arts and crafts show in a Minneapolis conference center downtown. Between sets he wandered, looking at the booths. He stopped at hers, "Selene's Silver Spoon Jewelry." As he admired the rings and bracelets that she had made from recycled silver spoons, he noticed how her smile lit up her face, then seemed to make the whole room happier. One thing led to another, and soon they were spending all their free time together.

After things got bad, Sam had tried to explain to Selene that his gigs were planned months in advance—months before he met her. He couldn't just cancel because she wanted to spend Valentine's Day together or because it happened to be her birthday. This was his career, the money he enjoyed making most—way better than his job stocking shelves at the Seward Co-op. Playing music made him feel alive.

But she wasn't buying it. Selene, with her killer smile and long legs, dumped him via text after she met someone else at another craft show. In some ways, Sam didn't blame her, but still, it hurt. He missed her kindness, her laugh.

Sam drew his fingers through his straw-yellow hair that stuck out in every direction. He chewed more cereal, studying the Honey Sunshine box in front of him. *Damn Selene.* He was beginning to wonder if his condition was permanent. He was still getting gigs and the money was okay, but the Twin Cities audiences wouldn't follow him for long if he didn't come up with some new stuff. And his agent, Gary, was bugging him about another album to follow up his first.

Damn Selene of the silver spoons.

"Selene of the Silver Spoons." He knew that would make a good song title, but *meh*. He couldn't work up enthusiasm to do anything with it.

Damn Selene of the soft sighs, long blond hair, beautiful smile.

Sam closed his eyes, trying to block the memories coming to him, when he heard the shower turn on in the apartment next door. This was a pretty good apartment building on the West Bank, but the walls were thin. The neighbor's shower butted up against his kitchen; he suspected their plumbing was connected.

He also assumed his neighbor was a woman from the bright flowery couch and chairs he saw when she moved into her apartment last week. And they were modern flowers—geometric—not old lady flowers. He didn't know which person was the new resident since so many people were helping, and he hadn't run into her in the hall or anything to say hey.

Thank God she replaced Old Stella, who complained to the manager every time he as much as plucked a guitar string.

He chewed some more. Drank a few swallows of juice. Almost time to go to the co-op and arrange cans by size and color. At least it was a co-op and not some lame big-chain grocery store. He liked living and working on the fringes. Working for Walmart or some other big company wasn't his style. Plus, he got a discount on organic food.

Through the grinding of his molars, Sam heard something. It could be his radio. Had he hit the snooze button by accident? He stopped chewing. The shower water next door was the only sound.

Sam started chewing again and the noise—no, the music—returned. He stopped chewing. *Was that singing?*

Yes, it was singing. *Good* singing. Just the snippet of a melody—haunting and slow—a woman's voice in a minor key. His arm was resting beside his bowl. He watched as the hairs on it started to rise like wheat after a rain.

Then the singing stopped. Sam looked at his kitchen sink, willing the music to start again through the wall. After a few moments, it did. Just eight notes, which the woman repeated. Sam jumped up, spilling cereal and milk across the table. Heedless, he ran for his bedroom. A thin reporter's notebook lay on the nightstand beside his bed. He grabbed it and a pencil, and came back to the table, sitting on the dry side. He scribbled furiously, writing down the notes his neighbor sang.

He felt on fire—as if this were the first song he'd ever heard. The notes were wondrous, round, melancholic. His mysterious neighbor kept repeating the notes for a couple minutes—enough time for him to record the melody on paper. He could see himself playing the tune on his guitar—see it spinning out into a longer song, *easy*. Add a little harmonica riff in the middle. *Shit*, he hadn't felt this good in weeks!

The singing stopped and Sam looked at the kitchen wall again, noticing the time on the clock above the sink. *Crap*. Time to head to work. He stuck his notepad in the back pocket of his worn jeans and quickly sopped up the mess on the table with a rag that he threw into the sink.

He put on his favorite baseball cap, the red one with a big yellow corncob on the front, courtesy of some company that supplied his dad with his corn seed. He grabbed his bike, which was leaning next to the door.

Carrying his bike down the four flights of stairs was faster than taking the elevator, so he headed down and out into the bustling morning streets of Minneapolis.

DURING HIS FIVE-HOUR SHIFT at the co-op, more pieces of the song came to him as he hauled boxes of food from the storeroom out to their place on the shelves. He didn't have a title for the piece yet but knew it would come once he spent more time with it.

Sam vaguely noticed his coworkers were trying to talk to him, but they gave up when met by his distant stare. Later, he overheard a couple of the new girls whisper something about him doing drugs. The other workers set them right. They said Sam was clean, he didn't do that crap. He was just working on a song in his head.

Sam smiled.

He usually worked mornings, saving afternoons and evenings for songwriting and gigs. He left the co-op at one, after buying some organic convenience food. He shoved it in his backpack and biked straight home.

More pieces of the song came to him while he was riding. He climbed the stairs to his apartment as fast as he could with his bike on his shoulder, barely noticing the people he met on his way. He dropped the bike inside the door and almost ran to the kitchen table, pulling out his notebook.

He finished the melody in stops and starts. *Now for the words.* He paged back in his notebook where he kept phrases that came to him upon waking, or that he overheard people say on the street or at work. He looked for words that fit the song's rhythm—*the shower lady's song*, as he now thought of it.

He stopped and listened, straining his ears to hear anything next door. It was quiet. Of course, she was probably still working. It was only early afternoon. Still, he kept an ear tuned for her as he wrote, curious about her schedule.

Since nothing was coming together with the words, Sam took a break to balance his checkbook and the money that bounced out as fast as it bounced in. Always living on the edge.

Later, as he was finishing his supper of garlic bread and organic canned spaghetti, the words came to him. It was like they sifted through his head from all the words he'd heard or thought about earlier in the day. They fell out onto his plate like dried beans.

"Oh baby, why'd you sail away and leave me, stranded on this shore? Baby, oh baby why don't you say you love me anymore?" And the rest followed.

MONTHS AGO, AFTER OLD STELLA had started complaining, Sam moved his practices from his apartment to the dust of his friend Randy's garage. Randy and his wife lived only a few blocks away, so it was easy for Sam to ride his bike to their place, guitar slung on his back, whenever he had the urge.

Randy had given him the key code to the security panel on the garage door. Sam would sit on a folding chair among the smells of street gravel and grass clippings, experimenting with the shower lady's song; moving out of the way when Randy or Melissa needed to park their car.

Sam soon started playing "Stranded," as he ended up naming the song, at his performances. Audiences liked it. So did his agent, who was excited that Sam was finally producing something new.

"More," Gary said. "Gimme more like that, Corn Boy, and you'll have enough for another album in no time!"

"Corn Boy" was Sam's nickname, a nod to his previous life with his dad and younger brother on the corn tundra of southern Minnesota. Plus, Sam's hair was the color of corn silk, and there was that cap he liked to wear. But his respectable stage name was Samuel Collins.

Sam *did* give Gary more. During the next couple of weeks, his neighbor kept singing in her shower. Every few days she offered a new snippet of a tune. Almost every time, the melody struck Sam and inspired him. Those days passed in a pleasant creative haze. His memories of Selene grew hazy and distant.

Back at the apartment, Sam had tried to catch a glimpse of his new neighbor—listening for her door to open—still trying to figure out her schedule. Other than her shower during his breakfast, he didn't hear her over there. He didn't hear her come home at night, which he suspected either meant she worked late, or that she had someplace else to go after work.

Maybe a boyfriend's house? He didn't want to think about that. He'd rather think of her as his own secret muse, just on the other side of the wall . . . .

THEN CAME THE MORNING when the shower lady's shower didn't turn on. Then another, and another.

Sam listened intently for any life next door, even putting his ear against the wall.

Nothing.

He began to wonder. Maybe she was in there hurt, maybe a victim of foul play, maybe in jail? No, not in jail. That didn't fit Sam's image of her. To him, she was young, modern, with long hair, and dewy skin from the shower . . . .

Several newspapers were strewn across her sunburst doormat. Sam wasn't sure what to do. Ask a neighbor? Nah, that would seem stalkerish. Besides, he didn't know any of the other neighbors.

"What do you think I should do?" he asked Randy the next time he was practicing in the garage.

It was Sam's third day without the shower lady. He didn't tell Randy that the woman was his muse, just that he was worried.

Randy leveled his brown-eyed gaze on Sam. "Why don't you just ask the landlord or the building manager?"

"You know they hate me," Sam said. "I've already got a bad rap with them from Stella. If I ask about this lady, they'll probably think I just want to case the joint or something."

"Yeah, but how are you going to find out about her otherwise?" Randy asked.

Sam searched the nooks and crannies of his muse-starved mind. Nothing came to him. He had to know what happened to her. What if she had moved? He had to find her. "I don't know. Guess I'll just have to put on my big boy coveralls and get to it."

Randy gave Sam's shoulder a fist bump. "That's my Corn Boy."

The next day, after another morning with silence next door, Sam knocked on the building manager's door on the first floor. The last time he spoke to Bruce, the manager had threatened Sam with eviction. Sam waited, holding his breath. A short heavyset man with graying hair opened the door.

"Whadda you want?" Bruce asked.

Sam paused, exhaling to keep himself calm. "It's my neighbor."

"Which one, 413 or 417?" the short man asked.

"413."

"What about her? She complaining about your noise, too?"

Sam shook off his annoyance. "No. I'm worried about her. Newspapers are piling up outside her door. I haven't heard anything over there in days. Could you take a look?"

Before answering, Bruce eyed Sam up and down as if searching his baggy T-shirt and jeans for drug paraphernalia. A sly smile slowly lit his chubby face. "Neighbor? What neighbor? That apartment has been vacant for weeks."

Sam's thoughts wheeled for a few moments, finally settling in the direction of ghosts. Bruce's smile widened at the expression on Sam's face. Sam's blood pressure spiked. "Cut the bull. She might be in there hurt or something. You need to go investigate."

Bruce's smile disappeared. "Just having a little fun. Let's go have a look-see." He closed the door most of the way and went back inside his apartment, returning with a set of keys. "C'mon," he said, and the two climbed the stairs to the fourth floor.

The newspapers were still lying outside the door of apartment 413.

Bruce knocked. When there was no answer, he took the keys from his pocket and opened the door. "You stay out here."

Sam obeyed but couldn't help trying to see inside. Her apartment was laid out differently than his. She had an entry hallway. His door just opened up into his living room. He saw an entry table with a lamp on it. A ceramic bowl—maybe for keys—sat next to the lamp.

Bruce's muffled voice came from inside. "I don't see nothin'. Don't see her. Wherever she is, I gotta leave a note letting her know I was here."

"So now what?" Sam asked after Bruce came out and locked the door.

"I'll call her work. Jane's a nurse at the county hospital—in the baby unit. Lives here by herself."

Sam's heart gave a jump. *Jane.* Now he had a name to go with the singing. And a profession. He liked that she was a nurse. It was a caring and respectable career. Bruce was on his way back down the hall before Sam collected himself enough to say, "Let me know what you find out."

Bruce just kept walking. His "Yeah, whatever" floated down the hallway.

THE NEXT EVENING was Friday night. Sam had checked his cell phone all day, hoping for a message from Bruce. No such luck. The wait was wearing on him.

As he ate his grilled cheese supper, Sam considered calling Bruce. He disliked the man, but how else was he going to find out what happened to Jane?

Bruce answered on the third ring, sounding annoyed.

"I was wondering what you found out about my neighbor." Sam didn't want to call her "Jane" to Bruce, sure that the way he said her name would give away his feelings. Besides, her name seemed too precious to utter to this jerk.

"Yep," said Bruce.

Yep?! Sam thought. *That's all he's going to give me?* "Well?" Sam asked.

After a pause, the manager said, "She's under quarantine."

It took a moment for Sam to process the strange word. He knew what it meant, just not the *why* of it. "So, what's the deal?" he asked.

"She was exposed to that new disease goin' around," Bruce said. "You know, that crypto-whatever-it-is. So, they got her locked in the hospital until they know for sure if she's got it or not."

Sam had heard of crypto. News reports said it stood for cryptofungosis, a nasty disease that was spreading overseas. It was caused by inhaling a fungus from the soil, but it could be passed from person-to-person, too. Pregnant women infected with it gave birth to babies with deformed arms and legs.

"How'd she get exposed?" Sam wanted to know.

"Dude, they wouldn't tell *me* that kinda thing," Bruce said. "All I needed to know was where she was at, and now I know, so I didn't go axin' all kinds of questions."

"Okay, okay." Sam tried to mollify the manager. "Thanks for telling me. Let me know if there's anything I can do."

"What *you* can do…" the manager said, "is to keep down the racket. Even if one of your neighbors ain't home no more."

Sam didn't think that deserved a reply. He pressed "end call" and looked at the wall behind his kitchen sink—a wall that Jane should be behind.

He had to get outside and think about what he should do. Sam left his half-eaten grilled cheese on his plate, slinging his guitar case over his back and his bike over his shoulder. He headed for Powderhorn Park, a couple miles down Cedar Avenue.

As Sam biked through traffic, the face of his mother floated in the humid summer air and green hedges before him. She was wearing her camouflage gear, looking at him with her soulful brown eyes. She had been a medic in the Gulf War. The helicopter she was in crashed; her body burned in the desert. They didn't have much to bury when she came home. It was like she disappeared when she walked out of their farmhouse door for her tour of duty.

Their dad had tried to hold it together for Sam and his brother, but things were never the same after their mother's remains came home in a gray metal transfer case. Dad threw himself into working the farm and never did find anyone else, at least not yet. Sam doubted he ever would, especially since he hardly ever left the farm.

Sam shook his head to keep the hollowness in his soul from growing. He kept pedaling. Once at the park, he leaned his bike against his favorite bench that overlooked the big pond in the middle. The water was full of goldfish, carp, and all kinds of plants or animals that people didn't want in their aquariums anymore. But Sam liked seeing the bright flashes of orange as the fish came to the shore, looking for handouts.

He sat on the bench and took out his guitar, strumming it absently. A breeze cooled him. The sky was beginning to take on the purplish hues of a watercolor twilight. What should he do? Jane, *his* Jane, might have some god-awful disease. He wondered how quarantine visits worked. Tomorrow was Saturday. He didn't have a gig or work. Maybe he should try to visit her—see if she needed anything.

That would be stupid. A girl like that probably had lots of people looking out for her. He'd just be in the way. What was he to her? Just the stranger next door. Then again, the hospital wasn't that far away. He could easily bike there or walk. Jane was probably pretty bored.

What if she died and he never got to see the woman who haunted him with her music? He could never forgive himself, never repay her if he didn't see her. It would be like his mom—like she left one day and never came back.

Jane should know the gift she'd been giving him, and how he'd been using it. Sam laughed at himself. He was getting all emotional about a woman he'd never even seen. He thought again about how she might look. With such a beautiful voice, she had to be beautiful.

What if she wasn't?

What the fuck did that matter? It was the place where Jane's music came from that he was falling for. That's what was important—the place inside her that he owed a debt to. Not her looks.

A couple wandered past and did their best to ignore Sam, until he started playing "Stranded." They stopped a few steps away and watched him play. The setting sun behind them created purple and red fuzzy haloes around their hair.

They clapped when he finished. Sam gave them a quick salute.

THE NEXT DAY, SAM CHAINED his bike to a lamppost outside Hennepin County Medical Center and entered, searching for the birth center. He knew Jane wasn't there but hoped someone could tell him where to find her.

The desk nurse at the center directed him to another building across the street. As he walked down the hall of the building, the smells of disinfectant and the silence of the closed, and presumably locked, patient doors unnerved Sam.

A dark-skinned woman sat behind the unit desk. She was talking on the phone but interrupted her call when she noticed Sam standing in front of her. "What can I do for you, honey?" Her voice had a southern twang that enchanted Sam. Her nametag read "Gladys S."

"I'm looking for Jane. I don't know her last name, but she's an employee here who's in quarantine."

Gladys spoke into the phone and ended her call. "You immediate family?" She looked Sam over.

He started to fidget, shifting from one foot to the other. "Not exactly." He quickly added, "But I'm her neighbor. I figured she might need something. I just want to help."

Gladys' gaze turned stony. "I can only let in immediate family and medical personnel." She paused for a moment, then maybe his hangdog face got to her. She said more softly, "It's too bad you ain't immediate family, 'cause nobody's been to see that poor girl other than some of her friends who are nurses. I don't know where her family is, but they shore ain't here."

Sam wondered why her family wasn't around. He also noticed the nurse didn't say anything about a boyfriend. He cleared his throat. "Well, can you at least tell me how she's doing?"

"No can do," said the nurse. "Only . . ."

". . .immediate family and medical personnel," Sam finished for her.

Gladys stood and peered across the desk at Sam more closely. "Say, ain't chu that musician? I thought I saw you at the 331 Club a coupla weeks ago."

"Yeah, that was me." Sam's heart gave a little hop. "Listen, I just want to see her. Just for a bit."

"You go in there and you gotta suit up like a Martian," Gladys explained. "Only her family can do that. Poor girl's in there for another three days till they know for sure whether she's got the crypto. Sorry, but I can't let you in."

"Well, can I at least call her or something?"

Gladys squinted her eyes. "She know you?"

" . . . No," Sam said.

"You two never met? What you doin' here then?"

Sam shrugged and tried to look innocent.

Gladys took his measure yet again. "You best approach her more careful-like, then."

He waited for the nurse to explain.

Gladys looked up at the ceiling for a moment, as if the answer were there. "Like . . . send her a letter or somethin'. Let her decide if she wanna talk to you. She under a lot of stress, you know."

"Thanks Gladys," Sam said. "That sounds like a good idea."

"Okay, you go on now. I 'spect I'll see you back here soon."

"I 'spect you will." Sam gave Gladys a smile.

JANE TURNED OFF THE TV gameshow and looked out the window of her hospital room. Rain sputtered, painting the windows with gray stringy rivulets. It was Sunday, and she had another two days left in this hellhole. That was, if she didn't have crypto. If she did have it, she'd be in for another two weeks, pumped full of strong anti-fungal drugs.

Jane sighed, thinking back to the chain of events that brought her here. It had begun with Christine, a pregnant woman who had just returned from a trip to the Middle East. When Christine felt sick, she had visited her doctor at the HCMC Birth Center. Jane was the one who had taken her blood samples and stood close enough to breathe in the air that Christine breathed out. Too late for Jane, the doctors had discovered that the cause for Christine's malaise was cryptofungosis. Now Christine was quarantined just down the hall, too, undergoing treatment and no doubt worried about her unborn baby. Even future babies she might have could be born with the deformities that were hallmarks of the disease.

Jane shuddered. Her foot stuck out from under her sheets. Although she was afraid of what she might see, she couldn't help but glance at her toenails, looking for any black streaks—one of the first signs. *Nope, nothing yet.*

Even though the disease was treatable, the medications were so strong that doctors wouldn't prescribe them unless they knew for sure she had it. So, Jane had to wait. She looked back up, catching a glimpse of herself in the mirror on the other side of the room from her bed. Her black hair that framed her straight brows and dark blue eyes was starting to get stringy. She hadn't showered in a few days.

Normally, she had a nurse's instincts to keep clean, but it's not like she had to shower to look good for visitors. She was an only child. Her parents lived on the West Coast, too poor to afford a trip to Minnesota on her mom's salary as a waitress. Her dad was a disabled vet from the Afghan War, and his disability check didn't cover much. Jane had come to Minnesota in search of a good nursing education, leaving the Oregon poverty behind. She'd gotten her degree, her first job, and now this . . . .

Thank God she had her cell phone—her one link to the outside world and to her parents. She also called her nursing school friends, who had all dispersed to other cities and hospitals. The few other friends she made here were great when she needed help moving, but most were too busy to visit her in the hospital. Or maybe too scared.

A knock sounded on the hallway window to her room. The staff used the tray underneath the window to transfer food and other items to her. Jane got out of bed and walked over to it. Gladys stood, holding an envelope in her hand.

"Sweetie, a man named Sam who says he's a neighbor of yours brought this for you." She held up the manila envelope, wrinkled with rain spatters.

"You mean from my apartment building?"

Gladys nodded.

"But I don't know any Sam," Jane said.

"Why not just read this and see what it says?" Gladys placed the envelope in the tray and pulled the lever that pushed the tray into Jane's room.

Jane retrieved it. "All right then, thanks." She turned and sat back down on her bed, ripping open the envelope. There was something hard in it besides the paper, but she ignored the object in favor of the letter.

Dear Jane,

Hi. I'm Sam from #415. I noticed you haven't been home for a while, so I got Bruce to check on you. Sorry to hear you might be sick. I saw on the news where that lady exposed a couple of other people besides you, and they're also under quarantine. That's got to suck.

You must be pretty bored. I'm including one of my CDs for you to help pass the time. I'm a musician and these are my songs. Not to freak you out or anything, but I noticed that you like to sing in the shower. I can hear it from my kitchen. You're a good singer, you know. I ended up writing a couple of new songs based on your tunes. Maybe someday you'll get out of there and I can play them for you.

I tried to visit you, but they wouldn't let me since I'm not family. So, this letter will have to do for now. But if you want, you can call me. I'm usually home in afternoons during the week (612-555-1234). Hey, maybe I could play my new songs for you over the phone!

Anyway, I just wanted to thank you for the inspiration, and to let you know that somebody's rooting for you out here. Give me a call and let me know how you're doing.

Your friend,
Sam

Jane laid the letter on her bed and took the CD out of the envelope. She studied the photo of the man holding a guitar and standing in front of a gritty urban scene. Sam was cute—with scruffy blond hair, deep-set eyes and a hint of mustache over his lip. His body looked wiry and tall, his fingers slim and nimble on the guitar strings.

A pleasant shiver went through her. *This* was her neighbor? Damn, too bad they didn't meet before she got quarantined! She didn't know how she felt about him overhearing her singing in the shower. That *was* a little creepy. She thought she was singing in private. The intrusion made her feel exposed. She crossed her arms and sat back against the pillows.

So, Sam had heard the little tunes she made up and had created songs from them. Should she be mad at him for "stealing" her shower songs? Jane thought for a few moments. *No.* She wasn't mad. She rather liked that something good came from the thin walls in her bathroom. She certainly hadn't been singing in the shower in the hospital since she got quarantined—she was too worried.

Jane thought back to when she used to luxuriate in her morning showers. Her singing came in fits and starts—only when she was happy and relaxed. She'd never had any vocal training. The songs just arose spontaneously. She had wondered why music sometimes came to her in the shower and sometimes not, until one day she had been curious enough to Google it. She discovered that shower singing had been scientifically studied, which made her chuckle. The researchers found that people liked to sing in the bathroom because the hard surfaces created good acoustics. "The multiple reflections from walls enrich the sound of one's voice," the researchers said. "Small dimensions and hard surfaces of a typical bathroom produce various kinds of standing waves, reverberation and echoes, giving the voice fullness and depth."

But that didn't explain the emotions behind it. Another link on "How Stuff Works," provided her with that. It said that people sang in the shower because they're alone, and they feel safe and comfortable in the warm water. "Stress literally washes off you. When you relax, your brain releases dopamine, which can give your creative juices a jumpstart."

The website also said that the act of singing made people feel even better because the breathing involved in it put more oxygen in their blood. This provided for better circulation, which improved their body and their mood. The result was something like meditation.

Jane had hardly taken any showers here. Not only because she didn't have many visitors to look good for, but because she was fearful of what she might see on her body once it was naked—black streaks on her skin and nails. If she didn't look at her body, she could ignore her current situation. Ignore the smooth white skin waiting to betray her.

How could she even think of calling Sam and starting a friendship when she didn't know if she was sick or not? But damn, she was lonely. She didn't know if she could make it the next two days while she waited for the news. She'd already called her family so often, and her nurse friends. It might be nice to talk to someone new.

Jane looked out her window at the rain still coming down. Sam must have braved the storm to bring her his letter. She smiled and kept mulling.

ON MONDAY EVENING, Sam just finished supper when his cell phone rang. "Jane Johnson" showed up on his caller ID. His heart went still at the unfamiliar name. He hoped it was his Jane. He swallowed hard. "Hi, this is Sam."

A moment of silence followed until the voice behind his songs spoke. "Hi Sam, this is Jane."

He didn't know what to say but quickly opted for cool and casual. "Hey Jane, thanks for calling! I guess you got my note."

"Yes. Thanks for the CD. I liked listening to it. You probably hear this all the time, but you're a really good musician."

"Well, I'm back to *being* a musician again, thanks to you." Sam felt trapped in the simplicity of his words. There was so much more he wanted to say.

"Oh, I'm sure it's not just me. You would have gotten inspired some other way, even if you hadn't overheard me in the shower."

Sam thought about this. She might be right. Something or somebody else might have inspired him down the line. "But the thing is, I *did* hear you and you *did* inspire me." He told Jane how he felt weird about it and had tried to meet her in their building.

"Don't feel weird," Jane said. "I think it's cool that something good came of it, especially now . . . when things are so uncertain . . . ."

"About that . . ." Sam didn't want to call the disease by name, especially since she hadn't. "When do you find out?"

Her answer came quickly, "Monday."

"Wow, tomorrow. If you don't have it, do you get to leave right away?"

"Probably not until Tuesday. It depends on when my doctor is at the hospital to sign off on the paperwork. The CDC is pretty strict about that stuff for quarantine release."

Sam didn't want to ask the next question and possibly upset her, but he needed to know. "And how long would you be in if you do have it?"

Jane sighed. "Another couple of weeks."

"That sucks. Let's hope for the best, then."

"You got that right. I'm about ready to tear my hair out as it is."

"Hey, want to hear one of your songs?" Sam asked.

"Of course, I do!"

"Okay, I'll go grab my guitar. And I need to sing quietly because the neighbors—not you, of course—get upset when I sing."

Jane laughed.

"Hey, can you video chat with your phone?"

"No, sorry. My phone's pretty basic."

Sam swallowed his disappointment. "Okay. Hold on." He got his guitar and sat on the couch. He switched on his phone's speaker.

As he began singing "Stranded," Sam noticed a quiver in his voice. Although he had performed the song in front of audiences half a dozen times already, this was different. This was *Jane*.

He stopped and cleared his throat. "Sorry," he said, taking a second to regain his composure. He continued, his voice stronger than before. Afterward, Jane was quiet for so long, Sam thought they'd been disconnected. "Jane?" he ventured. "You still there?"

"It's beautiful," she said. "I can't believe you got that out of something you overheard from me. I've never even been in a choir."

Her voice was soft, and he couldn't quite tell what emotions were behind it.

"I think I'd better go," she said. "Someone's coming in to take my vitals. Six times a day, every day. Doesn't even matter if I'm sleeping. But they're earlier than usual tonight."

Sam caught a hint of disappointment in her voice. "Oh, okay," he said, although he didn't want their conversation to end.

"You got my phone number to call back?" she asked.

Sam brightened. "Yeah, it's on my caller ID."

"Okay. Give me a call tomorrow night. I should know by then."

Sam hesitated. "Okay," he said. "I'll call you. Hang in there, you hear? I'll be here whatever happens."

Jane's voice softened again. "Thanks. I appreciate that. I'll talk to you tomorrow."

"Okay. You take care and rest easy now."

"I will. Bye."

Sam wanted a few more moments on the line with her, so he waited before saying, "Bye Jane. And good night."

TOSSING AND TURNING THAT NIGHT, Sam had an idea. Early the next morning before his shift at the co-op, he rode back to the hospital and bought a teddy bear for Jane from the gift shop. It was tan and plump. Smiling, it held a red heart that read "Get Well Soon."

Poor Jane; today was D-Day. He hoped to God she didn't have crypto, both so she could avoid further isolation—and because he wanted to see her and meet her in person as soon as possible.

The question of her appearance still nagged him. As he walked down the hallway to her unit clutching the bear, he thought about asking Gladys what Jane looked like. But any way he worked out the request in his head sounded weird and shallow. He reminded himself that it was the place inside her that her songs came that mattered.

When he arrived at the nursing station, Gladys wasn't there. Sam left the bear with the other nurse on duty and asked her to give it to Jane.

Work was unbearable. He mixed up brands of organic kidney beans on the shelves, put kale in the green onion bin, and got reprimanded by his boss for forgetting to close the storeroom refrigerator door completely. He should just go home. How was he going to survive the next few hours? Shit, how was *she* going to? He hoped the teddy bear would help. It seemed so lame, but it was the best he could do for now. He was so scattered and stressed, he couldn't even channel his feelings into a song.

After narrowly surviving his bike ride through the traffic, Sam arrived home. He couldn't eat. Instead, he paced his living room floor until he thought it was a good time to call Jane: 7 p.m. His heart raced as he punched her contact listing on his cell.

She answered after the second ring with "Hey Sam."

He tried to divine her emotions from her greeting. She almost sounded relaxed. "So, what's the news?" he asked.

"I don't have it!"

Sam couldn't speak for a few moments. "Oh, I am so happy to hear that!"

"You and me both," she said.

Sam thought he heard her bouncing on her bed. "So, when can I spring you from the joint?"

Now it was Jane's turn to pause. "Would you mind bringing me home?"

"Hell yes!" he said. "If you don't mind."

"I'd like that." Jane's voice had gone all soft. The sound melted something in Sam's belly. "Anyway, I don't have my car here because I took the bus to work. My car's parked in front of our building."

In his enthusiasm to bring Jane home, Sam conveniently overlooked that his bike was all he had to offer for transportation. He felt like an idiot, but an alternative came to him quickly. "Hey, I don't have a car either, but I'll pick you up in an Uber."

"I'll hold you to that." After a moment, Jane added, "Guess what I am hugging right now?"

"The bear?"

"You got it. He's my favorite visitor so far."

"I'm glad to hear that. I figured you would need something to hug today, either way."

"I still can't quite believe I don't have crypto," Jane said. "After I found out, I said a prayer for all those poor people who do. I felt guilty to be so relieved when they're suffering."

"It's all right, Jane. The only one you can do anything about now is yourself."

A moment of silence passed over the line. "You're right," Jane said. "Hey, I'll see you tomorrow, Music Man. Will 9:00 work?"

"Perfect," Sam said, liking his new nickname already.

AS SAM RODE IN THE UBER the next morning, he thought about the fitful night he'd just spent wondering about Jane. He wasn't sure how he'd react when he saw her for the first time. From their phone conversations, he'd built a clearer picture of her in his head—more than just the long hair and dewy skin he'd imagined before. Now he imagined her eyes, colored with compassion, and brown hair. Her voice didn't sound encumbered, and he wanted to believe it came from a graceful neck and through smooth lips.

He wanted to be attracted to her, but *what if,* when he saw her in just a few moments, he wasn't? He knew himself well enough to understand that he would be disappointed if he wasn't. In that case, maybe he and Jane could just be friends. Would that be enough? Would he still gain inspiration from her once he knew what she looked like?

For a few moments, he thought about turning around, not meeting her. Maybe it was better not to know what she looked like. That way, he could maintain his vision of her—not have reality intrude. He could just tell the driver to do a U-turn.

No. Jane would be disappointed if he weren't there to pick her up. He needed to go through with it. He needed to meet this woman, no matter what. If he wasn't attracted to her, it wouldn't be the end of the world. And why should the world revolve around him, anyway?

Sam watched the trees laden with green leaves slip past outside the car windows, his eyes shielded from the sunbeams by his corn seed cap. Selene flitted through his mind. Had he ever felt this strongly about her? Would he be willing to rearrange his gig schedule for Jane's birthday or for Valentine's Day?

Honestly, he was willing to do just about anything for this woman. A spike of nerves made his stomach clench. Soon, the Uber pulled up to the hospital doors. Sam instructed the driver to wait and he got out. As he walked through the doors and down the hallways with their locked rooms and harsh smell of disinfectant, his stomach rolled into an even tighter ball.

His mother's face, vague and brooding, seemed reflected in the curtained windows. He took off his cap and stuck it in his back pocket, drew his hand through his wild hair.

Finally, he saw Gladys standing behind the nursing station desk. She smiled at Sam. "C'mon honey. Let's go get Jane outta here."

They walked a few doors down and Gladys opened Jane's door.

A Night in Biosphere 2

Monsoon winds drifted across the desert, bringing curtains of rain to the thirsting land. One night late in September, a severe storm passed over the tiny town of Oracle, an hour out of Tucson. A lightning bolt struck a building. Not just any building—one of the "Lungs" of Biosphere 2.

The Lungs were built to equalize air pressure in this experimental three-acre enclosure designed as a mini-Earth. Eclectic and idealistic, the builders of Biosphere 2 thought of Earth and its various habitats as Biosphere 1. Their creation was designed to test whether humans could live on Mars or some other planet. With more than a bit of grandiosity, they dubbed it as the second biosphere.

Most of the Biosphere 2 buildings featured glass walls and ceilings, except for the two Lungs. With their white and dimpled geodesic domes, they looked for all the world like giant golf balls half-sunk into the desert. The Lungs kept the glass structures from exploding or imploding from temperature and air pressure changes inside and out. Only one was working. After the whole of Biosphere 2 was built in 1987, the owners discovered that the South Lung was enough.

Inside that Lung, a rubber diaphragm circled the fifty-foot-high ceiling, connecting the steel walls to a huge aluminum dish suspended in the center. The dish acted as a counterweight to the air swirling in and out of the Lung through several tunnels connected to the other buildings. Multiple metal support posts ringed the dish's edge, giving it the look of an alien spaceship from a 1950s horror movie. As air pressure in Biosphere 2 increased, the 40,000 pounds of rubber would expand, raising the dish. As the pressure decreased, the rubber would shrink, and the dish lowered until its spaceship legs settled on the cement floor.

Cut into the floor below lay a circular pool of water that served as a reservoir. It collected condensation and overflow from the facility's irrigation system, and it provided 200,000 gallons of water in case of fire.

The searing bolt struck the middle of the South Lung, snaking down one of the metal supports, into the water. The electricity sparked flecks of pollen that had floated into the pool on the Biosphere 2 wind from plants in the Rainforest Mesocosm, dead skin cells from workers and visitors, amino acids aerosolized from the spray of the Ocean tank's mechanical waves, and years of detritus collected in the soup of the pool.

After two quasi-successful experiments in human isolation, the Biosphere was now open to the public—a local tourist attraction designed to generate revenue for upkeep. After changing hands several times, it was now owned by the local university and also functioned as a research lab.

Visitors on the hourly tours thought Biosphere 2 was just a museum or a science center. Harmless and nerdy.

But lightning struck. The pool glowed. And a new form of life . . .

Began.

WE ARE HUNGRY. The insects that fall into our pool are no longer enough. As we grow, we need more protein to build our form. We are a collective, like one of the sponges attached to the rocks in the Ocean beyond. Because we are made of all, we know every being—plant and animal—in this place.

We need protein to evolve, grow, walk outside the pool, form muscle, search out more protein.

We stretch, the clear glue of us rising above the tensile surface of the water, open to air. The air is more friendly to us now. We like to breathe, absorb it into our cells. The land air is richer than the dark water oxygen, more complex, fragrant.

When the humans come, we lie still, clear in the pool except for a few bugs suspended in our insides that we haven't yet digested. The people think the bugs are just drowned, floating in the water column. Nothing unusual.

Many people pass by every day. We are growing larger. Hiding is getting harder and harder. Soon, we will need to leave the pool for our life on land. But first, we need the protein.

We wait. We wait for our chance. We are so, so hungry.

One night, our chance comes. We can smell him, salty and meaty. He's near—in one of the tunnels that connects the Lung to the rest of our world. He's alone, not moving. This is the first time one has stayed here at night. There's just one. Vulnerable.

We consult, gather, push ourselves over the edge of the pool. We slide across the prickly cement, working together.

Out, at last.

CHASE ANDREWS GROANED. He raised his hand, felt the slick of wet blood and the goose egg on his forehead. He didn't dare open his eyes for fear it would hurt.

The last thing he remembered was walking at the end of the Biosphere tour line, up the slope of one of the narrow, dark tunnels away from the Lung. He was lagging behind the group, checking his phone. The battery was dying, and he was waiting for a text back from Charlotte, the cute girl in his biology class.

Although his battery still had some juice, he couldn't get any reception. Maybe all the cement was the problem, plus the tunnel was underground.

That's where his memories stopped.

Lying on his side with his eyes still closed, Chase carefully moved his arms and legs. He rolled onto his back. His ribs ached on the side where he must have fallen. Other than confusion and having a splitting headache, he seemed good to go.

Chase opened his eyes. Darkness gathered around him like hungry coyotes. A dim light down the corridor showed he was still in the hallway. He listened, only hearing the hum of the machines that operated the Biosphere.

Shit, he must have been out for a long time. He'd taken the last tour of the day for extra credit for biology class. What if everyone else was gone? Slowly, Chase sat up and felt for his phone. It lay a few feet to his right against the wall. He grabbed it and pushed the activation button. Nothing. He messed with it some more, to no avail.

Shit again.

Chase looked up and saw what must have been his downfall: a low doorway, oval and steel, like those on submarines. He touched his forehead again, winced.

He arose and started walking back to the Coastal Fog Desert Mesocosm, following the multiple pipes that lined the hallway walls. Along the way, he wondered how the tour guide could have left him here. Didn't they count everyone when they exited the Biosphere? Perhaps the guide had been in a hurry to get home. Still, it was no excuse to leave him wounded in the hall.

As Chase rounded a corner, he fought the rush of air that swept from the other Biosphere buildings to the Lung. His eyes watered. Wiping the moisture away, he noticed a lighted sign where another corridor joined the main one: "Emergency Phone." He didn't feel like he needed to use it just yet. Maybe a door would be open and he could just walk out, get into his car, and drive back to his dorm. With momentary panic, he felt around in his pockets for his car keys. Still there.

In shape from skateboarding and taking kids in the Camp Wildcat program on overnight mountain hikes around Tucson, Chase extended his lithe pace. His university sponsored the camp to help underprivileged school children get out into nature. He was one of the counselors when he wasn't studying.

Chase carefully ducked through the low doorways until he reached the Coastal Fog Desert, which was under glass. He hoped it might be brighter, with more lights. But of course, it wasn't. The builders had wanted to mimic nature as much as possible, which meant only light from the waning moon was available to guide him through the Joshua trees with their prickly arms reaching for the sky like people under arrest. He could just make out the winding trail. Each step jarred his head and compounded his ache.

Nevertheless, Chase started to lope; he wanted out of this place. It was so creepy at night. Near the juncture with the Savannah, he stumbled and brushed one of the plump round barrel cactuses. A sharp pain lanced through his calf. He yelped and stopped, gingerly extracting the long spines. God, he wanted out of here. He tossed the spines away from the trail and took off again at a slower pace. The Mangrove Marsh was on his right, its trees and their interconnected roots tangled like a nightmare of mixed-up computer wires. The marsh gave way to the Ocean, which sloshed restlessly below a high walkway through the Savannah.

When he was about mid-Ocean, Chase took a right through a door into the Human Habitat. The biospherians, as they were called, lived here during their experiments. He entered on one of the darkened top floors, loped through the kitchen and found the central stairway. He raced down it, twisting his ankle, adding insult to his cactus-injured leg. He gingerly put weight on his ankle, wincing. He could still use it if he was careful.

Finally, Chase was at the front door. He paused, breathing hard. He tried the door. It was locked. Although he knew it wouldn't help, he wriggled the handle vigorously several more times and then hit the door with his free hand in frustration. Why would they lock the doors from the inside? Maybe some other door was open. He remembered seeing an exit door in the Rainforest Building during his tour. He limped back up the stairs to find it, taking a left when he reached the Ocean walkway.

The Rainforest was separated from the Savannah by a rubber-sealed door with strips of hanging plastic. As he opened the door, air heavy with moisture and the smell of green enveloped him. The sound of the manmade waterfall tumbling down fake rocks roared in his ears. As he made his way to the outside door, the feelers hanging down from the trees seemed to try to hold him back. He shrugged them off and found the door. Also locked. Fear began to tingle up his backbone.

Chase fought the urge to bang his head against the door. *Why, why locked?* Then he remembered the human experiments. The first group of biospherians were locked inside for two years. The Biosphere owners probably didn't want to change the locks in case they needed to hold similar experiments in the future.

Triple shit!

Chase tried his phone one more time. Still dead. He would need the emergency phone. He made his way back to the Lung tunnel, entering the even narrower passageway where he'd seen the phone sign. His footsteps echoed off the metal pipes.

Who should he call? His roommate? Nah, Darren passed up the opportunity to go on this extra-credit trip in favor of a party tonight. He was probably zonked out in bed by now. His parents? Nah, they lived half a continent away in Wisconsin, and they were probably asleep, too.

Should he call 911? Maybe. He had a medical issue, right? Several. A lighted rectangular phone box jutted out from the wall. Hmmm. It didn't seem to have numbers you could dial, only an on-off button. Was it hardwired to 911? Chase picked up the receiver and punched "On." After static, a few clicks sounded. When he heard a ring, he let out his breath.

"You have reached the Biosphere 2 Visitor Center. For tour hours, press one. For conference facility information, press two. For reservations, press three. For all other requests, please stay on the line for our receptionist."

A sinking feeling grew in Chase's stomach, which also growled with hunger. He stayed on the line, praying that a real person would answer.

"You have reached Biosphere 2. Our hours are Monday through Saturday from 9 a.m. to 5 p.m. We are closed on Sundays. We are currently closed. Please leave a message and someone will respond as soon as possible."

Shit all around!

A beep sounded and Chase panicked, trying to decide what to say. "Uh, I'm Chase Andrews. I was on a tour today. I got hurt and was left behind in the Lung hallway. Now, I seem to be locked in. I'd sure appreciate it if someone would come let me out. I'll be . . ." he struggled for words, ideas. "I'll be by the door where the tours start—in the Human Habitat. Please hurry."

He hung up and leaned against the wall, the back of his head resting on the cement blocks. He'd better go back to the front door, and do what? Wait.

Chase trudged to the main hall. When he reached the junction, the breeze in the tunnel seemed to switch directions. A strange smell wafted to him—like tuna or maybe a can of freshly opened sardines. *Weird.* Then he heard a low slippery sound, like something gliding across the floor. It came from the direction of the Lung. He looked but couldn't see anything in the gloom.

He took off toward the Human Habitat door as quickly as injuries would allow. He tried the door again and it was still just as locked. With nothing else to do, he sat in the tiled entry with his back to the wall. He leaned his head on the door and tried to sleep—ignoring the throbbing in his head and leg.

He'd taken biology because he wanted to be a scientist, maybe a medical researcher. He wanted to understand how things worked—wanted to help people. He'd better get triple extra credit for this tour.

THE HUMAN IS MOVING. We were too slow—too unused to gliding on land—to catch him while he was lying still. We follow. Along the way, we find a small, furry mouse in the hall. We extend our sticky foot and encircle it, gradually making the circle smaller and smaller until we catch the being. It squeaks and squirms, but we engulf it and bring it into ourselves. After a few jerks, the mouse quiets, suspended inside us like the bugs, and we slowly digest it.

We extend our slippery foot, quickly making our way to larger prey, following his scent. We find him at the bottom of several flights of stairs. He is not moving. We hide, suspended by our sticky foot from the ceiling until we are sure he must be asleep. Slowly, we glide down the wall and start to feed on one of his feet.

CHASE WAS GETTING SUCKED DOWN and down in the nightmare quicksand, the air slowly crushed from his lungs, the sand rising from his feet to his chest. Now it was making its way up to his neck . . .

He awoke with a start and a yell, heart pounding. He breathed hard, relieved to find his chest unencumbered. The strange fishy smell was back, and it was strong. His uninjured foot felt weird—wet and stinging like the time he stepped on a jellyfish at the beach. He looked down to see his foot engulfed in a clear spongy jelly. The emergency light over the door showed him things were trapped inside the gel: a mouse, a cricket, a bunch of flies—like a vat of aspic gone wrong.

Chase screamed and stood on his bad leg, trying to stamp the thing off his foot. Each time he stamped, the jelly fluoresced a luminescent blue. "Help, help!" he yelled.

The thing was about four feet long and two feet thick—shapeless, faceless—a giant amoeba. Chase fought the urge to grab it with his hands. He and Darren had just watched *The Blob* during a Halloween monster movie marathon. He feared if his hands got stuck in the stuff, he'd be a goner. The teens in the movie had defeated their nemesis by spraying it with fire extinguishers. The movie blob hadn't liked the cold spray. Maybe that would work on this one, too?

Chase remembered seeing an extinguisher around the corner on the wall. He threw himself in that direction. Immediately, his bad leg buckled, and he fell hard to the tile floor. His bruised rib muscles spasmed. Once he caught his breath, he looked down toward his engulfed foot to make sure his other foot wasn't in the stuff. It was free.

He struggled to make his injured leg work again, ended up crawling over to the extinguisher, dragging the heavy beast with him, barely able to make headway. He supported himself on the wall, stood and hefted the CO_2 extinguisher off its hook. The blob was nearly up to his knee now. Panicking, he hit it with the extinguisher. All that did was make it glow again.

Chase took a moment to collect his wits and try to figure out how to make the extinguisher work. He popped the pin, aimed the nozzle at the blob, and pushed a button. The white cold mist hit the blob. Chase expected it to squeal, but the blog simply shrank and retreated, taking his shoe with it.

Chase dropped the empty canister and ran up the stairs as fast as his gimpy leg would allow, through the kitchen and into the rainforest. His flight was a primitive impulse. He'd always been good at climbing trees. Maybe he could get away from the blob that way. He found a large tree with smooth bark and branches low enough for him to grasp, but high enough, he hoped, that the thing couldn't reach.

He scrambled up about twenty feet and rested on a large branch, panting. Both of his feet and legs hurt now. His head still pounded. Soon, he could hear and smell the blob approaching. The cold and the closed Rainforest door hadn't deterred it for long. It stopped at the tree base, moved a few inches ahead, then back again. It began to surround the tree with itself. The blob stretched up the trunk until it left the ground. *Damn, the thing can climb!*

The blob seemed to climb slower than it had glided across the floor. Chase knew he needed to do something soon or he'd be trapped. He looked for a branch from another tree that he could use to escape. No such luck. He made his way down the tree trunk toward the clear, glistening glob. It was about a dozen feet off the ground now, steadily advancing.

Just before he would have had to touch the thing, Chase jumped down and away from the tree. He landed on his good leg, twisting his ankle and falling. He stifled a yell, not wanting the thing to know he was hurt. He could hear the slimy sound of the blob changing direction, coming back down.

Slowly, like an eternal nightmare, Chase arose, moving as quickly as both bad ankles and a shoeless foot would allow, lurching like Quasimodo. The thing was sure hungry. Hell, *he* was hungry. He ran for the kitchen, inwardly cursing the people who decided to change the Biosphere's agricultural area into a research facility once the human experiments were done. If they had left the garden, he could have had some food.

Once he reached the kitchen, Chase propped a chair against the door, hoping to slow whatever gross, overwhelming thing was chasing him. He flicked the light switch on the wall, hoping . . . success! He opened the fridge. Only a bottle of juice stood inside. He opened the freezer. *Yes!* A bunch of frozen steaks lay inside. He grabbed them, placing them on the counter. He popped one into the microwave and set it on defrost. Although he was famished, he figured he would feed the blob first. And defrosting the meat would make it more appetizing to a thing that didn't like cold.

He could hear the blob at the door, see its clear gel covering the upper window as it tried to find a way inside. After a few minutes, it cracked the window and came for him. At that moment, the microwave dinged. Sitting high on a stool behind the kitchen counter, Chase threw the steak at the floor in front of the blob. He held his breath. The blob stopped, seemed to sniff the meat, then gradually engulfed it. Was it Chase's imagination, or did the blob turn opaquer as it ate the steak? It seemed whitish now, more solid. He didn't watch for long, placing another of the five steaks in the microwave, praying the meat would defrost before the thing started looking for him again.

Just as the microwave dinged, the blob advanced. Chase threw the steak again and repeated the process. He wasn't sure what he would do once the steaks were gone. He looked around the kitchen for another extinguisher, anything. Then he noticed the stairway up to the biospherians' bedrooms. If those doors didn't have any windows, maybe he could barricade himself inside.

As he watched the blob eat the third steak, he could see it was definitely growing whiter, larger, and more upright. What was happening to this thing? And where had it come from? He was certain only of two things: he was trapped inside here with it, and he was going to keep feeding it no matter what so that it wouldn't eat him.

After the last steak, the blob stopped advancing. Now taller than wide, the blob stood at about the height of a twelve-year-old child. Taking advantage of the blob's stillness, Chase grabbed the juice from the fridge and limped to the stairway, crawling up the stairs on hands and knees to take pressure off his ankles. He limped between the three rooms, trying to choose the best to barricade himself inside. Thankfully, none had windows in their doors. The middle one looked good; it contained a small bathroom, several chairs and a dresser, plus a window to the outside that maybe he could use to escape.

Chase glanced down the stairway, expecting to see the blob coming after him any moment. Instead, it climbed back up the kitchen door and out through the broken window. He didn't pause to ponder his good fortune but hobbled to the middle bedroom and pushed the dresser across the carpet against the door. Once satisfied the door was secure, he tried the window. It had no handles or knobs. He swore. Of course, there'd be no way to open it. The whole point of the Biosphere was self-containment. He looked out into the dark night. Away from Tucson, the stars shone like a luminous cape across the sky. His longing for the freedom of the outdoors was palpable; he could almost taste the desert dust.

He made his painful way back to the door, putting his ear against it, listening for slithering. All was quiet.

The clock on the wall showed midnight. Leaving the light on, Chase climbed onto the bed and opened the juice bottle. Between gulps, he tore sheets to wrap his angry purple ankles for support and to reduce the swelling. He elevated his legs on pillows and took off his remaining shoe, dropping it to the floor. Having his feet at uneven levels was doing more harm than good.

Revived by the liquid, Chase's brain began working better. After about twenty minutes, he realized that if the blob came for him in this bedroom, he had no defense. He should go back to the kitchen and look for a fire extinguisher. Slowly, painfully, he hoisted himself out of bed and removed the furniture from the door. He opened it a crack, looking left and right. No blob within sight or smell.

Chase hobbled downstairs and searched the cupboards and walls for an extinguisher. He finally found a small one in a cabinet under the sink and slowly made his way back to his room, repeating the barricade.

He lay back down on the bed, heart pounding, fire extinguisher by his side.

SATED AND THIRSTY, we retreat from the human, back to our watery home to drink and rest. We will search for him again, later.

WHILE HALF-HEARTEDLY trying to sleep, Chase had ample opportunity to think. He wondered what the blob was, where it had come from, where it had gone. It was like nothing else he had ever seen before—like some land-based amoeba that could move and climb with its pseudopod. And now it was growing larger. What was it going to grow into? Like an amoeba, would it divide in two? He shuddered, fervently hoping he was not here long enough to find out.

As a biology major, Chase felt guilty he was not more excited about this find. Maybe the blob was something totally new. But damn, the thing had tried to eat him, he was sure of it. Maybe biology and research weren't all they were cracked up to be. This whole Biosphere facility was devoted to a biological experiment and look what happened—it had most likely created this nightmare creature.

His tired mind wandered into hallways of human hubris. What did people think they were doing, trying to recreate the Earth under glass? The human experiments here hadn't really worked. There'd been too little oxygen for the biospherians because the designers hadn't taken into account the amount used by the curing concrete walls or the amount used by soil microbes. They'd had to pump in tanks of oxygen into the South Lung. They'd also had to let one of the biospherians out of the facility soon after the first experiment began for a medical procedure that the crew doctor couldn't perform.

Chase wondered if he should switch majors from science to something more social. He enjoyed working with the kids in Camp Wildcat—the way their faces lit up when they discovered they could pitch a tent for the night or climb a mountain. What if he wasn't cut out for medical research? What if his life's work lay in a career that helped people more directly?

Oh man, changing majors would mean more time in college and more student loans. With paying out-of-state tuition, by the time he finished college he was going to be at least $80,000 in debt. He couldn't imagine adding to that.

He felt a tired grin cross his face. This was all assuming he survived the night. He needed to survive and *then* he'd figure out the ramifications. His roiling thoughts suddenly focused on one fact: by feeding the blob he'd made it stronger and larger. Chase clutched the extinguisher closer, like a cold metal teddy bear through the eternity of the wakeful night.

At about 8:45, Chase carefully made his way to the door and listened. Silence. He cracked it open and looked around. Nothing. Extinguisher in tow, he made his way down the stairs, his ankles even more painful now, his forehead crusted with dried blood. He looked out the broken kitchen door window. All was quiet. Where was the blob? He turned and walked through the Human Habitat, down the stairs, back to the front door.

Chase watched the visitor center atop the hill for any signs of life. He saw no movement. It must be 9 a.m. by now. Where was his rescue? He limped over to the tour orientation room. The clock there said 9:10. He went back to the front door.

With a terrible sinking feeling, Chase realized today was *Sunday*.

As he turned to find shelter, the smell of sardines wafted toward him.

Dedicated to my college-age son Hunter, and to Russell, my dream man, who gave me the ending for this story.

The Stolen Stories

The house in Brigantine, New Jersey, waited, eternal and patient. Strips of white paint were peeling off the front of the two-story Cape Cod, a victim of salt air. Its faded green trim had withstood the sun of twenty summers and was now the same color as the dry grass in the front yard, but the dwelling was far older than its trim paint.

The house hugged the street. People passing never gave it a glance. If they had paid attention, they would have noticed the structure listed a bit to one side like a tree shaped by coastal winds. Its large back yard sloped gradually to an alley. From the attached garage on the rear of the house, a driveway ran to the alley. A rusty gray dumpster sat to one side of the driveway.

The house expected Joey to visit as he had for the past few weeks, almost every day. Joey was the grandson of Clark and Melinda, the people who left and never came back.

Soon enough, the cold metal of a key intruded into the front door lock. The house opened its vision to the outside and saw Joey, felt the warmth of his hand grasping the doorknob.

As Joey opened the door, stale air that had collected inside wafted past him. He slouched through the living room, past the antique card catalog in the corner. His tennis shoes, dusty from the five-block walk from his house, left a trail across the dull green carpet. He entered the kitchen, flicked the light switch, and sat at the round wooden table, looking at the mound of boxes he had been sorting through.

Joey and his father had boxed almost everything up in the kitchen for donating to Goodwill before realizing they could make money off the antique china and implements. Now, Joey was sorting through the boxes to see what might have value while his father worked at the casino.

The house felt the air stir as Joey sighed in the yellow kitchen. It remembered Joey when he was young, his laughter and curious energy bouncing off the walls, filling the empty places built by his quiet grandparents. Now, he was sullen and impatient, so different.

Joey opened the nearest box and rummaged through it. Metal clinked upon metal. He pulled out a small silvery gadget with a hand crank attached. His brow furrowed. "What's this one for?" He leaned forward in his chair and pulled his cell phone from his back pocket. He took a picture of the device and pushed more buttons on his phone for a minute or two.

Joey set his phone and the unknown thing aside on the table and kept sorting through the box. Soon, his phone chimed. He picked it up, looking at the screen. "Oh, an eggbeater. Why couldn't they just use a fork?"

As he texted back, he whispered the words as he spelled them, "Thanks, Bobby." Then he shook his head and tossed the beater into a large box on the kitchen floor. "Guess I can eBay that one. Looks antique." He reached into the box again, repeating the process with more kitchen tools, although he recognized some without Bobby's help.

Joey's cell rang. The house remembered the fizz that used to pass through the line in the walls whenever the landline rang for Clark and Melinda. Now that phone didn't ring.

Joey reached for his phone on the table, squinting at the caller's number before answering. "Hey Dad," he said. "Yeah,

I'm at the house. I'm workin' on it." All was silent for a few moments while Joey listened. "No, I don't have a job yet... whatd'ya want me to do, clean up this junk or get a job? It's kinda hard to do both at the same time." A few seconds passed. "Well, I'm tired afterward, and all the places are closed. I can't just ignore my friends, ya know." Another moment passed. "If you'd give me my data plan back, I could apply for jobs online. It's not like Grandma has Wi-Fi. Plus, I could look up all this junk. I dunno what half of it is." Silence for a while, then, "But, like I said, I'm tired when I get home. Last thing I want to do is get on my computer."

A short time later, the house heard him make a sound that could have been a curse. "Yes, I'm goin' as fast as I can. I'm not sure how much longer it's gonna take, especially without a data plan. Just be glad I'm doin' this and not you. And you should be glad I'm not wastin' any more of your money at college."

Joey grimaced. After a strained silence, he said, "I don't care how hot the housing market is now—there's no way I can finish up in one week. Grandma and Grandpa have fifty years' worth of stuff here. You've seen it! The soonest I could do it is two weeks, plus you give me my data plan back."

Joey listened to his father for a few more moments, then said, "I know you coulda hired a cleaning service instead of me. Okay, it's a deal then. Ten days and the data plan. I gotta get back to work." He punched a button and tossed the phone onto the table. He continued rummaging but was quieter now.

He finished sorting one box and stood, picking up another off the floor where he'd been throwing things that were broken or not eBay-able. He opened the back door and a fresh breeze from the ocean a few blocks away slipped inside, lightly misting the dark hickory woodwork. He walked partway down the gravel driveway to the dumpster and tipped the box's contents into it. He re-entered the house, carrying the empty box. Instead of sitting at the table, Joey carried the box into the living room, turned, and went upstairs.

The worn wooden stairs creaked and groaned under Joey's weight and the house shuddered a little. It could feel the smooth slide of Joey's hand along the grooves in the railing.

At the top of the stairway, Joey passed several full bookshelves lining the hall. He stopped to gaze at the worn books his librarian grandmother had collected, pulling out a few, thumbing through the first pages.

"Huh, *Treasure Island*, third edition. *Moby Dick*, second edition. Bet these will bring in more dough than that kitchen junk. Maybe I'll save the best for last," Joey said. Then softer, "Sorry I didn't pay more attention when you tried to read them to me."

The house knew Joey must be talking to Clark and Melinda. Joey continued walking and turned to the right, into their bedroom. The house remembered when Clark disappeared. He'd been coughing, so Melinda took him to the hospital. He never returned to the house or to his job managing an Italian restaurant in Atlantic City.

A few years later, Melinda was in the kitchen cooking Sunday dinner in preparation for a visit from Joey and his dad, Richard. She fell over and never got up. By the time father and son arrived, the oven was smoking. Richard turned it off before anything, but the pot roast burned.

Strangers came and took Melinda away. The house could still smell the faint ash on the kitchen wallpaper, which sported images of steaming pots and vegetables. The house felt a pang of indirect desolation at their absence, like it had with all its former owners who had died or left over the years.

Then the quiet had descended, only broken by Joey's visits. Would new people arrive to live inside it like before?

Joey went to the closet that held Melinda's clothing. He dropped the box nearby and pushed the hangers back and forth, going through dresses and shirts. Then he turned and walked to the bed, grabbing a paper grocery bag lying on it. He brought the bag over to the closet and started stuffing clothes into it. Some went into the box on the floor, hanger and all. "What the fuck do I know about women's clothing?" he muttered.

He filled the first bag and opened another. After he was done, he left, carrying the overflowing box. Once outside, he emptied the box of clothes over the dumpster's side. He kept the box again, and brought it inside, dropping it on the kitchen floor.

Joey walked into the living room and sat on the dark gray sofa. He pulled out his phone and typed on it. Soon, it rang. "Yeah Bobby, I'll meet you there. I'm done here for now. This place gives me the creeps, anyway. See ya in twenty."

He shuffled across the carpet and the house felt the hard key in the lock. Silence returned.

THE NEXT DAY WHEN JOEY ARRIVED, the house woke again. Joey began working in the kitchen, made a few trips to the dumpster, and then went upstairs to the bedroom with its wallpaper of faded red roses. He finished sorting through the clothes in the closet despite phone text interruptions. Later, he worked on the rows of shoes from the closet floor and the items stacked on the upper shelves.

Joey opened hatboxes, old camera bags, and a shoebox full of letters. He took his time with the shoebox, reading the envelopes and taking out a few pages. "Huh, Grandpa wrote these." He read aloud, "My dear Melinda." Then he rolled his eyes. "How *sweet*."

After Clark's death, the house remembered Melinda carefully reading each letter every month or so. Her eyes would mist over as a wistful look crossed her face. She would place the envelopes gently back into the box for the next time.

The house watched as Joey tossed the letters back inside the box, returning the cover and putting it on the bed.

"I suppose Mom will want to see those, if she can ever stop bangin' her new boyfriend long enough." Joey snorted. "Mushy girl crap." Next, he took down a worn leather bag. Its brass buckles were spotted with tarnish and a large handle rested between them. Brass hinges on either end made up the rest of the bag's large mouth.

The house remembered when Clark brought the bag home, years ago. Melinda, curious, asked him what was in it. Clark closed all the curtains in the living room before sitting down on the couch to show her. He put the bag on the coffee table. "You can't tell anyone, but I got this for you from a guy who knows a guy . . ." Clark had whispered.

"Honey, why are you whispering?"

"This is big stuff."

Melinda spoke more quietly. "How big?"

"The biggest." Clark opened the bag and Melinda peeked in. She took out a few sheaves of paper and began to sift through them.

"Is this what I think it is?" Melinda's voice rose in excitement and concern.

Clark just nodded.

"But how did you . . . how . . . where in the world?"

"I can't tell you, but they're yours now, darling."

Melinda sat back on the couch; her face drained of color. "But the world's been looking for these for decades—ever since his first wife lost them on a train in Europe. Or they were stolen. They're all his early works! No—no, these are too valuable. We can't keep them here."

"That's precisely *why* we're keeping them here. This is the last place anyone would look."

The house watched as Joey set the leather bag on the bedspread and sat next to it, fiddling with the buckles. Finally, he was able to unclasp them and pry open the stiff hinges.

He looked inside. "Just papers," he muttered. He took out a stack and read one yellowing page: 'The Dark Horse, a short story.' After a few moments, he dug deeper into the bag and pulled out a letter. "'Dear Mister Hemingway, we regret to inform you that your story does not meet our needs at this time.'"

Joey looked closer at the letter. "Huh. Dated 1915. Shit, this stuff's old. I wonder if it's valuable." He looked up at the ceiling as if he were thinking. He shook his head and dug through the bag some more. In a quick motion, he pulled out his hand, peering at the black smear on it. "What the. . . ?" Gingerly, he reached into the bag again. "What's this black crap?" He took his hand back out and rubbed it on his pants. "At least it comes off." A dim light dawned behind his eyes. "Oh yeah, a carbon copy. I remember hearing about those." Joey rummaged through the papers some more. "Another rejection letter from 1922. This guy musta been a real loser. Why would Grandma keep somethin' like this? It's not like her books."

Joey's phone rang, distracting him. "Hey Bobby. What? Yeah. No, I can go. This is so boring. Hey, I gotta question for you." After a moment, "Yeah, I'll be there in fifteen."

Joey left the bag open on the bed and went downstairs. Locking the front door, he departed.

THE NEXT DAY JOEY CAME BACK, carrying tape and a pile of large, padded envelopes. Cool salty air trailed him inside. He sat on the gray sofa and played with his phone for about an hour. Later, he got up and went into the kitchen. He had finished sorting through the initial boxes he and his father had packed. Now he was classifying the remaining contents of the shelves and drawers, putting them into their respective boxes and making trips outside as necessary.

He lifted items out of the eBay box and sealed them into the envelopes for mailing. After he had a stack of about a dozen, he went upstairs and started working on the chest of drawers in the bedroom. Joey took several bags of old socks and underwear out to the dumpster. The house saw him look at the sky on his way back inside.

"Better finish up soon today. It's gonna rain. I forgot my raincoat for walking home. I'm gonna get drenched. Damn, I can't believe I gotta get this done so fast—only eight more days. This rain couldn't have come at a worse time." Joey walked back upstairs and finally turned his attention to the leather bag. He reached into it again. "Papers and more papers." He pulled out another letter. "Look, another rejection. Bobby says he ain't hearda no Ernest Hemingway. Nobody wanted his stories. LOS-ER. I don't have time for this." With that, Joey picked the worn leather bag off the bed and hauled it downstairs and into the back yard.

The house watched as he threw the bag over the side of the dumpster, fading sun glinting off what shine remained on the buckles. The bag landed atop the junk at the bottom with a thud.

Joey came inside. He sat on the couch and played with his phone. After a while, he looked up, noticing a light rain pelting the windows. "Done for now. Storm's comin'." His words hung in the empty air. Joey rose to leave.

The house felt the front door close. Later, the wind picked up. A massage of rain fell harder on its roof.

In the back yard, yellowing pages flew, twirling above the dumpster and scattering across the lawn.

The house was the only witness as rain glued the paper to the grass.

Dedicated to everyone who has cleaned out a relative's home, and to Ernest, whose stories were never found.

Invisible Connections

Sheila watched as a woman lifted a book to her nose and inhaled, a smile blooming. Sheila shook her head. What was it about the smell of books? People's reactions were always the same—that slow smile.

From her desk in the spacious reference section on the library's second floor, she could see patrons scattered across the room, reading books lying open on the tables before them.

Can't get that smile from a Kindle. What would people do if books were all electronic? Sheila hoped that day never came. She loved the feel of paper in her hands.

Jason approached, pushing an overflowing book cart. He wore the button-down shirt and dress pants required by the library's attire policy. Jason was about her age, in his late twenties. He started working at the library a few weeks ago, and so far, she liked him.

"You read *The Overstory* yet?" he asked.

Sheila nodded. "Yes, I learned so much about trees! Thanks for recommending it."

"I thought you'd like it, Nature Girl." Jason smirked, using the nickname the other staff members called her.

With an air of mock indignation, Sheila said, "I prefer Eco-Babe, if you don't mind."

They muffled their laughter, not wanting to disturb the patrons.

"What did you think about the whole trees communicating thing?" Sheila asked.

Jason ran a hand through his brown hair. "I'm skeptical. Trees talking through their roots, and even through the air with chemicals? That makes for good fiction, but I think that's all it is." He paused. "I mean, if trees were that smart, wouldn't we have noticed by now? I think Richard Powers just has a good imagination."

Sheila frowned. A few weeks ago, when she was still in dating mode, she would have hidden her opinion to win his favor, but she was taking a break from dating and was done with hiding her opinions. Her silence made men think she was someone else. She was through being a pretty face with a personality put on to please others. What had that ever gotten her? One failed relationship after another.

Sheila recalled a quote mistakenly attributed to Einstein: "The definition of insanity is doing the same thing over and over again and expecting a different result." She would stand up for what she believed, but she needed to tread carefully. Sharing opinions was one thing, totally alienating a coworker was another. "Reading *The Overstory* totally changed my dog walks," she said.

Jason raised an eyebrow. He leaned over his elbows on his book cart, waiting for an explanation.

"Every day, I walk Cubby through the woods near my aunt's—" She paused to correct herself. "Near my house. There's a trail that leads into Wickham Park. Those walks have changed how I think about trees. I feel different afterward—better. It's like . . . what if that's because the trees have communicated with me somehow, influenced me?"

Jason's gaze was cautious, not exactly encouraging her to continue, but not shutting her down, either.

"You know, I'm always picking up litter and using canvas bags instead of paper bags. Sometimes I wonder if this whole sustainability thing wasn't my idea." Sheila adjusted her glasses. "What if all the time I'm spending with the trees is making me do it?"

Jason laughed. "Ooooh, sorry for chaining myself to this bulldozer, officer, the trees made me do it!"

"Well, who knows? Look at what happened in the book. The characters tried to save the redwoods because the trees drew them out to California to do it. What if the trees are influencing me without my knowing it?"

Now it was Jason's turn to look upward in thought. He leveled his gaze back on her. "You don't really believe that do you? Trees can't make you turn into an environmentalist. No way."

"Would that be such a bad thing?" Sheila said. "We—humans—think we are so powerful and in control. What if we are more connected to nature than we think? What if something mysterious is happening that we don't understand? And what if it's not just me? What if it's . . . a lot of us?"

Jason grinned. "Intriguing ideas, but I can't say I believe them. If they make you feel better, go ahead. Maybe you should stop walking in the woods if it's freaking you out so much."

A chill ran through Sheila. "Oh no, I couldn't do that! Besides, Cubby loves it. The forest is about the only place I can let him off-leash—no cars. He's always sniffing something or chasing squirrels."

"He doesn't run away?"

"No, he's too much of a mama's boy for that. He rarely goes farther than twenty feet from me. He always needs to be near." Sheila often wondered if this behavior was linked to what happened to Aunt Miranda. After her aunt's death, and the distraction of the subsequent news media frenzy, the poor dog had been trapped in the house for two days before anyone thought to check on him.

Jason started walking away, pushing his cart. "Gotta do some shelving. Later!"

Sheila watched him walk down the aisle, trying not to let his dismissal bother her. Her thoughts roamed to her dog walks. The one place she avoided during them was "the house." She shuddered as she recalled the nondescript gray structure where her Aunt Miranda lost her life, only a few blocks from her house. Even though a new family lived in the gray house now, Sheila preferred to walk Cubby through the parking lot behind the school so she wouldn't have to pass the place.

Although she didn't want to go over it again, the reel of images spooled through her mind—the lurid TV news stories: "Home invader shot by father protecting disabled son," "Home invader, elderly neighbor," "Police seek answers in recent home invasion."

The police had questioned Sheila: what was her aunt's state of mind lately, did she have a habit of wandering into neighboring homes, did she have dementia? Sheila could offer no answers. She didn't understand why her aunt broke into that house—why she would want to intrude in the dead of night on a boy with that awful syndrome. Sheila had been so caught up in her own daily stresses—her mother had suffered a stroke and was in the hospital—that she hadn't seen Aunt Miranda in weeks.

Even after Sheila moved from her apartment into her aunt's house, she found no clues to her aunt's behavior. How could she have done something so horrible? Sheila remembered fondly how her aunt and uncle used to take her on camping trips as a child in their VW van. They all had such fun hiking together, and her aunt and uncle had taught Sheila the ways of the woods.

She shook her head. She'd better finish looking up a patron's information request. She sighed as she woke her computer from its temporary slumber. Soon, it would be time for lunch, and she could work on her jigsaw puzzle.

SHEILA AND CUBBY TURNED OFF the gravel road and onto the hiking trail. "Okay, Cubby, quit pulling . . . stay." The reddish goldendoodle stood still. Sheila reached down and unhooked the leash from his collar. He bounded ahead. She took a few steps and looked up to the treetops, fuzzy with green buds. Fog shrouded the forest, dimming the evening sun. She could just make out the top branches of the oaks and maples before the gray became impenetrable.

Sheila strode ahead, not wanting to lose sight of Cubby. The dog slowed, sniffing mosses newly free of snow, scrubby young pines, and scattered gray leaves left from winter. As she passed a wide spot in the trail where an old car wreck used to molder, Sheila checked for large pieces of glass—remnants from its windows broken long ago and beer bottles tossed out of its doorless sides by unruly teenagers of the past. The edge of a large, clear glass shard glinted in the soil. Sheila took a small stick and dug it out, pocketing it along with several others that rested on the surface. She felt like she was extracting a painful sliver from the forest floor.

Cubby lifted his head and looked back. Satisfied she was still there, he trotted on. A couple of robins trilled nearby.

As she walked over a small rise, Sheila reached out her arms. The cool mist coated her hands. She inhaled the freshness of spring. Peace descended upon her, pushing away the vague, persistent restlessness she always felt—like she should be somewhere else in the big wide world, but she wasn't sure where. She thought, *Is the peace from me, or is it from the trees?* Were they, even now, emitting pheromones and chemicals into the mist? *Are they making me feel this way?* Or was it something from the trees' roots? Did chemicals seep into the soil, only to be inhaled by her dog, or scuffed up by her shoes and launched into the air? Jason and his opinions be damned. She took another look at Cubby. Did he feel the peace, too? The dog stood about fifteen feet away, staring into the forest. In a flash, he took off.

Sheila walked to where Cubby disappeared. She could hear him running, but the fog obscured her view. As she stood, the sound of his running stopped. She expected to hear him bark, frustrated by a squirrel up a tree. A few moments passed. No barking. Unease crept in. Where was he? "Cubby? Cubby, here boy!"

She listened for a response. Nothing. Feeling alone, she looked up the trail as far as the mist would let her, searching for someone to help. Nobody. Sheila took a few steps off the trail in Cubby's direction. "Cubby, come!" Only silence met her command. This wasn't like him. "Cubby, come!" she called again.

The peace fled from her. She peered through the fog, straining to hear even the slightest sound. She kept walking into the forest. She was glad the shrubs and brush hadn't leafed out yet—it made the going easier. Aside from old leaves rustling under her feet on the forest floor, it was as if she were under a silent glass dome, cut off from the rest of the world.

She called Cubby again, to no avail. After taking a few more steps, Sheila arrived at a large maple with gnarled bark. It stood amid smaller trees like a sentinel. Instinctively, she reached out and touched the nubby trunk, slick with mist. She pressed her other hand to the bark. Nobody else was here to help her. So, she whispered, "Bring my dog to me . . . please." She hugged the tree, laying her cheek against the cool roughness. "Please bring me my dog. I need him."

In a few moments, she heard running feet through leaves. She peered around the trunk at a red blur streaking toward her. She stepped out from behind the tree. "Cubby!" She bent and ruffled the dog's ears. He gazed up at her, his lips stretched in a doggy smile.

"Good boy," she said, then more sternly, "What in the world were you doing?"

His gaze offered only innocent animal happiness.

"Come on." Sheila stood. "Let's go."

They found the trail and continued through the fog, propelled ahead by force of habit. Cubby was in the lead as usual, and as they walked, Sheila wondered at her actions with the tree. Where had the idea to hug it come from? And did it actually work, or was it just coincidence that Cubby returned after her silent plea?

The only way she could test it was if Cubby ran away again. But that behavior was so unusual, she doubted she'd get a chance to try. And why had he bolted into the forest in the first place? He usually barked at squirrels. Maybe the squirrel had disappeared into the fog or was so fast that it had already leaped into another tree. Or it was hiding behind the trunk.

Another thought occurred to her. What if the trees had lured Cubby away?

Sheila and Cubby topped a small rise in the trail. Sheila halted and looked around, trying to regain her lost sense of peace. A woodpecker drummed deep in the forest. Everything else was still—even Cubby, who had stopped when she did.

The dog looked at her expectantly. Sheila shrugged, and they continued.

Now her thoughts bounced in another direction. Just before Cubby ran away and she got distracted, she had felt a presence. Was it the trees? Something else? She didn't feel it now. An image of her Aunt Miranda came to her. Was it her aunt watching them? They weren't that far from *the house*. Because of her sudden death, was her aunt trapped in some woodsy purgatory, unable to leave the neighborhood?

The presence hadn't felt menacing. Indeed, it had been serene, uplifting . . . even curious, perhaps. If it was her aunt, she apparently meant no harm. But Sheila hadn't sensed her anywhere before, and from what little she knew of ghosts, she suspected she would have felt something before now. She'd been living at Aunt Miranda's place for close to a year.

It could be the trees—maybe it had something to do with her heightened awareness of them.

Sheila and Cubby were nearing the turnaround point in the trail, where it crossed a gravel road that led to a few scattered houses. Ahead, Sheila half-expected to see the super-charged creatures of air and light from *The Overstory*. The pattern of the mist revealed no humanoid shapes, however. Sheila shook her head at her foolishness and stopped at the road. Cubby investigated the greening low grass along its edge.

"C'mon, Cubby. Back this way." Sheila turned and pointed down the trail. The dog obeyed.

Sheila stopped. Did she really want to go back past the spot where Cubby ran off? No. Did she want to feel that presence again, if it wasn't that unsettling? No thanks. Dusk was falling and the woods were getting darker. If she took the road back home, at least it would have streetlights.

Cubby stopped and looked back at her, questioning.

Sheila turned. "This way," she said, stepping onto the road. As the dog neared, she hooked the leash onto his collar. This road would lead them past *the house*, but that seemed preferable to *the tree* for now.

They crunched down the gravel and took a left onto Woodlawn Drive, which led past the school and curved around to Sheila's street. Mist shrouded the scattered homes from view. She imagined what she and Cubby must look like to anyone peering out their window: two dark shapes, gliding past.

The tall white house where Ken lived came into view. Sheila had met him on eHarmony, and they went out a couple of times—the last at his house for dinner a few months ago. But during the middle of their date, Sheila realized the man loved hearing the sound of his own voice.

She could hardly get a word in edgewise around his detailed descriptions of his job monitoring bacteria in the city's wastewater treatment plant.

During a bathroom break, she arranged for her girlfriend Tina from the library to call her and give her an excuse to bail. Tina had sent Sheila a text pretending she was out for a bicycle ride and one of her tires got flat. Night was approaching and she needed Sheila to pick her up in her car and take her home. Ken believed it and even offered to help, but Sheila had brushed him off and escaped.

No lights glimmered in Ken's house. Maybe he wasn't home from his exciting job yet.

Sheila had had a few run-ins with catfishers on eHarmony, and quickly learned to stick with guys she knew were real and were local. While she was seeing Ken, she'd been dating two other guys. She'd enjoyed meeting them all, had fun. But they weren't deep relationships. She wasn't all-in. Some mysterious necessary ingredient was missing, as if she were a tree without soil, rootless and disconnected. She hadn't felt like she could let them see who she really was.

Perhaps sensing this, one of the guys had ghosted her. Sheila had let down the other two, including Ken, easy and quickly. She didn't want them to waste time on her, no matter how much fun they had together. She knew that dragging things out led to harder feelings at the end.

She broke up with them the hard way: in person. She thought that texting or emailing a breakup lacked respect. Doing it in person gave the guys a chance to ask her questions, get feedback, vent. That made things a lot less awkward if they ran into each other later. This town was small enough that such meetings were a possibility, yet large enough that they were rare. The men had taken the breakups well and even now, she and Ken waved when they happened to drive past each other in the neighborhood.

The breakups were exhausting, though. She'd deleted her profiles and was taking a time out for now. Or was she? The image of Jason and his friendly gaze flitted before her. Sheila shook her head.

Sheila and Cubby walked past the driveway of the house where the neighborhood policeman lived. He and his wife had walked down Sheila's street a couple of times, marveling at Cubby. One of the times they even chorused, "We love goldendoodles!"

Once, Sheila had been speeding home to grab concert tickets she'd forgotten, and the cop had stopped her a few blocks away. Not recognizing him, she'd given him her license without comment. After he checked it in his car and walked back to her open window, he said, "You're Cubby's mom, aren't you?" He let her off with just a warning.

Then came "the house." The new family had painted it a cheery pale yellow. They kept their curtains open all the time, allowing light to flood into the yard. She could see a hazy glow as she neared. Mounds of children's toys provided lawn topography—she could just make out a trike and assorted dump trucks.

Cubby stopped and looked toward the house, silent. After a few beats, he continued, pulling at his leash down the street and toward home.

Seeing life in the house made Sheila glad, but she always wondered if her aunt was still in there somewhere, too. *That's one mystery you'll drive yourself crazy trying to solve.* She shouldn't dwell. Sheila and Cubby took the curve and then turned right onto their street. She smiled contentedly as they walked up the driveway of the large cedar dwelling that was now hers.

SHEILA SLID A PUZZLE PIECE with a white star and dark blue background into place, locking with the knee of a red-coated Canadian Mountie. As Sheila took a bite of her turkey and cheese sandwich, Tina sat across from her at the library break room table, lunch bag in hand.

"You combining puzzles again?" Tina took her PB&J sandwich from her bag.

"Yeah. It's much more interesting than doing just one puzzle, don't you think?" Sheila looked up at her friend. "I got the Mountie from the Tweed Museum of Art and the space one from that kids' store, Skylark."

From the pile of pieces awaiting placement, Tina handed Sheila an edge piece.

"Hey, thanks!" Sheila added it to the pile of edge pieces she was amassing to her left.

"Whatever floats yer boat, Nature Girl," Tina replied. "How do you find ones with the same pattern?"

"I guess I've bought so many puzzles over the years, there's bound to be ones with similar patterns."

"How do you know which ones to combine?"

Sheila paused, then shrugged. "I must have a good visual memory or something. I just remember which ones have the same patterns. I mean . . . I spend so much time with the puzzles. The patterns just get in there." She pointed to her head and looked back down at the puzzle.

Tina took a bite of her sandwich and chuckled. "Hey, maybe you're a puzzle savant."

Sheila glanced up and then back to her puzzle, laughing. "There might be such a thing, but I don't think I am one."

"How do you know?"

"I'm a *reference* librarian." Sheila emphasized the word "reference," proud of her elevated status and pay in the world of library science—even though she knew that Tina already knew this. Their differing jobs at the library were a standing joke between them. Tina was a library technician, which offered lower pay and took less education. But they both knew Tina would make a fine reference librarian if that's what she wanted to do.

Sheila and Tina had been friends forever—growing up on the same street, concocting neighborhood adventures. Sheila was usually the instigator and Tina the willing accomplice, like the time they dug a small hole along a trail in a vacant lot. The hole was big enough for a foot. They planned to trip a neighbor girl they didn't like because they deemed her spoiled. Sheila had devised a plan for Tina to lure the girl to the trail with candy. But eventually, their anger toward the girl had cooled and they thought better of the scheme.

Tina smirked. "There you go again, with the reference librarian thing."

Nonplussed, Sheila listed by rote the qualities that distinguished a reference librarian from a technician. "Reference librarians have the people skills to provide good customer service. They play the part of dynamic guides—joining users on their journey to knowledge." Sheila knew if she looked up, she would see Tina mouthing the words along with her, but with a twinkle in her eye.

"How could I ever forget?" Tina added, "Hey, do you remember my friends Marge and Justin?"

Sheila added another piece to her puzzle. "The ones who moved to Oregon?"

"Yeah. You know how they were having trouble having a baby? Well, I just found out that Marge is pregnant!"

Sheila kept concentrating on fitting a piece of the Mountie's red uniform together. "Hey, that's great," she said, although the thought of having a baby seemed far away and alien. She supposed it was because she didn't have a boyfriend, which, of course, was step one in the world of human procreation. Justin and Marge's happiness only served to highlight her single status. Time to change topics. "Something weird happened to me in the forest by my house."

Tina looked at her expectantly.

"Cubby ran off, chasing something. It was that foggy day last week, and I couldn't see him. I called and called, and he didn't come back. That's not like him."

Just then, Jason arrived and sat down with his lunch. "Hello, ladies."

The women said hello.

"What's this about your dog?" he asked.

"He ran away in the woods," Sheila said. "Anyway, I ended up hugging a tree. This huge grandmotherly maple was nearby." She didn't like the quizzical looks on her coworkers' faces, especially Jason's. "Nobody else was around. I didn't know what else to do! So, I hugged this tree and asked it to bring my dog back."

"Did it work?" Tina asked.

"It seemed to. Not long afterward, Cubby came running back."

"Just a coincidence," Jason said.

"That *is* pretty weird," Tina said.

"The rest of the walk was fine. But we didn't go back home on the trail. I took the road instead."

Jason set his sandwich down and wiggled his hands on either side of his head. "Woo, woo. A little like *The Overstory*, huh?"

"I don't know," Sheila sighed. "I've thought about it a lot, and don't know what to make of it."

"Have you walked the trail since then?" Tina asked.

"Nope, too weirded out."

"Well, the only way to find out is to see if it happens again," Jason said.

"I don't want to. What if my dog never comes back?"

"How about if I come with you? Would that make you feel better?"

Sheila looked hard at Jason. Did she really want him getting any closer? She was doing just fine on her own. "I don't know." Besides, she didn't like his patronizing tone.

"You should become a tree researcher," Tina said. "This could be your first experiment. I bet you could get your PhD from it!"

"How could a person study something like this?" Sheila asked.

"Oh, I don't know," Tina said. "Maybe not. Besides, you're too cute to need a PhD."

Sheila frowned. "What *exactly* do you mean by that?" This was going off their private joke script.

Tina sat back. "I mean, PhD students have horn-rimmed glasses and big noses. You don't have either of those. *Geez*, it was a compliment!" Tina squirmed. "Did you think I was being sexist or something?"

Sheila said, "Yes!"

The trio sat silent. Jason was smart enough not to add to the discussion.

Sheila found another puzzle piece and slid it into place. "Thank you, I guess," she muttered, sitting back and taking a bite of her neglected sandwich.

After a few moments, Jason said, "You ever hear of those tracking devices for dogs?"

Sheila shook her head.

"They clip onto their collars. If your dog runs off, you can see where they are online in real time."

"You should totally do that," Tina said. "If Cubby runs off during your experiment, you'll know where he is just by looking at your cellphone."

Jason continued, "C'mon, Nature Girl, let me help."

Tina glanced sideways at Jason, then back at Sheila with raised brows. Sheila did not respond.

"I could set you up with the tracker and we could do the experiment," Jason said. "If Cubby goes missing, I'll help you search for him."

Sheila tried to think of a reason to dismiss the tracking idea, but she had to admit, it was a good one. Besides, her friends just wanted to help.

"Okay." Sheila sat back from her puzzle. "Let's do it!"

CUBBY STOOD LOOKING OUT the living room window at the driveway. Soon, he began barking. Sheila got up from the couch and saw Jason parking his car. She quickly rose and clipped on Cubby's leash, heading out the door. She wanted to meet Jason outside, so she didn't feel obligated to invite him in.

As Jason climbed out of his car, Cubby pulled Sheila down the back stairs and raced to greet him. The dog sniffed Jason's legs and pranced in excitement. Jason rubbed the dog's floppy ears and smiled. "Hey, I think he likes me!"

"I think he does." Sheila didn't have the heart to tell him that Cubby greeted everyone with equal enthusiasm.

"Nice place." Jason glanced at her house. "Big!"

Sheila shrugged. "Yeah. It took some getting used to."

"How many bedrooms?"

"Four. I inherited it from my aunt, along with her furniture. My own stuff would never have filled the place."

"Sorry about your aunt. But sweet deal on the house. Hey, I got the tracker." He held out a small blue rectangular device.

Sheila commanded Cubby to sit and Jason turned the tracker on and clipped it onto his collar.

"Let's test it first." Jason pulled out his phone. "I downloaded the app so it would be ready to go. It uses GPS so you can see your dog." He frowned as he studied his phone. "Why don't you take him down the street a bit."

When Sheila and Cubby were half a block away, a blinking yellow light on the dog's collar caught her eye. She looked back to Jason.

"Got ya!" he yelled. "You can come back now."

As Sheila walked up her driveway, she asked, "Did you turn that light on?"

"Yeah, it's got three types of lighting options: steady, fast-blinking, and slow-blinking. That way you can see him at night."

"Cool." Sheila leaned over, peering at Jason's phone.

"See, here you are now." He pointed to a circle on the screen that had other circles emanating from it, like a radar ping. "And you were here." He pointed to a spot farther away on the screen.

"That's good," Sheila said. "Thanks for picking it up. How much do I owe you?"

"Don't worry about it." Jason smiled. "It's all in the name of science."

Sheila did not like being indebted to Jason, but she wouldn't make a big issue out of it right now. Cubby pranced and pulled against his leash. "Let's go," Sheila said. "Somebody's getting restless."

They walked down the street and onto the gravel trail. The trees sported larger leaves. The air was clear, and a warm breeze rustled the lingering dead leaves of winter on the ground. Sheila unclipped Cubby's leash. "Well, it's not foggy like before, but we'll see what happens."

Cubby bounded ahead, stopping to sniff mysterious scents every few feet. He seemed glad to be back on the trail again. Sheila almost wished they were alone so she could feel the presence of the trees better. Jason was distracting.

"So, you said you inherited your house from your aunt," Jason stated. "How long ago did she die?"

"More than a year ago. It was very sudden. It came as a shock to us all." To distract him from further questions, Sheila asked, "Do you have any relatives in town?"

"Nope. I'm from Pennsylvania. They're all back there—my mom, dad, and brother. I came here for college. Liked it, so I stayed. How about you?"

"I grew up here. My parents still live here, too." As she spoke, Sheila kept track of Cubby. He wandered about fifteen feet ahead of them. "My mom had a stroke last year, but she's back home now and getting stronger every day."

"Oh man, sorry to hear about the stroke. Do you see them often?"

"Yeah, we get together every week. I help at their house, too. Something's always breaking, or they need lightbulbs . . . that kind of thing."

"You must be handy," Jason teased.

"If you can't be handsome, might as well be handy," Sheila said, quoting *Red Green*, a popular home improvement comedy show set in Canada.

Jason snickered, understanding the reference. "You have any sibs?"

"No, just me."

They walked over a small hill in silence, still keeping an eye on Cubby. The spicy smell of wild leeks wafted around them as they passed a large patch, their pointed green leaf tips emerging from the forest floor.

"Here's where it happened." Sheila stopped and pointed into the forest. "See? Cubby marched right by. Nary a sniff now."

"Well, we'll see what the rest of the trail has in store," Jason said.

As they continued, Sheila thought about how many times she'd noticed library patrons smelling books and then smiling. An idea struck her. Could tree pheromones be contained in and emitted from the paper? Could the trees be providing a feeling of well-being through the books, similar to what she got from hiking in the forest?

The concept excited her, but she didn't want to share it with Jason yet. Not after he and Tina had jumped on the idea of the trees influencing her dog. She wanted to think the idea through more before announcing it to the world—put her reference librarian skills to work on her own search. *The Overstory* didn't get into that territory. This idea was her baby, and she was keeping it to herself for now.

Jason bent and picked up a stick, studying it. "You ever think about continuing your education—doing the whole PhD thing like Tina was saying?"

"No, not really. I feel like I have the career I want. I am a *reference* librarian, after all. What higher aspirations could a person have?" Sheila smiled.

"Granted, I don't know you that well, but you have a questioning mind. Seems like you'd do well in a doctoral program."

In her surprise, Sheila almost stopped walking. She caught herself and kept going, saying, "I don't know how I'd pay for something like that."

"Maybe you could get some local botany prof excited about your idea about trees influencing people. They could take you on in a fellowship."

"Seems sort of far-fetched, but maybe."

"'Bout as far-fetched as trees talking," Jason quipped.

There it was again. This guy was brutal. As they neared the turnaround point in the trail, Sheila asked, "You want to take the road or go back on the trail?"

"Let's do the trail and see if Cubby reacts at that spot."

They turned around and walked back the way they came, conversing about work issues and gossip. During a lull, Sheila asked, "Did you hear that Hemingway's lost manuscripts were found?"

"No way!" Jason said. "Where?"

"In a dump in Jersey!"

"How'd they get there?"

"We may never know," Sheila said.

"What an awesome find. I wonder if they'll ever be published?"

"I would assume so. I bet those New York publishers are dying to get their hands on them, even though some of the pages are missing. Might have to pay the city dump a small fee, though."

The pair laughed, then Sheila stopped walking, watching Cubby intently. "Here we are again," she said, softly. "I'm not sure why I'm whispering. Just seems like the thing to do."

Cubby just kept walking, his gaze straight ahead.

"Oh well," Jason sighed.

"I guess we'll have to wait for a foggy day," she said.

"Yeah. I'll show you how to download the app. And I'll delete it from my phone so you don't think I'm stalking you guys." Jason stopped and pointed at her. "But when it gets foggy, you call me and let me help, okay?"

Sheila smiled at his earnestness. "Okay. Scout's honor."

DURING A SLOW TIME AT WORK, Sheila opened her web browser and typed "tree pheromones in paper." The first document she found was a story in *Smithsonian Magazine* about a German forester who believed trees could talk to each other. The information was similar to what the fictional botanist in *The Overstory* espoused. One quote from the forester caught Sheila's eye. He said, "They call me a tree-hugger, which is not true. I don't believe that trees respond to hugs."

Sheila snorted and then thought, *Maybe the trees don't like you.* She minimized her browser and glanced around to see if any patrons or staff were approaching. All was clear. She returned to her search.

Next came a blurb about what kind of trees are used to make paper. The rest were all variations on articles about how trees can communicate. Nothing about communicating *through* paper, though.

Tell me something I don't already know.

Next, she entered the same keywords into an academic paper search engine. Nothing. Then she went back to her browser and typed "why does smelling books make people smile?" A YouTube video came up describing why people love the smell of old books. It explained that smells are linked to memories. The International League of Antiquarian Booksellers claimed people like the smell of old books because of lignin—a compound in wood that smells like vanilla and is found in paper. Other pungent paper chemicals were benzaldehyde, ethyl hexanol, toluene, and ethyl benzene. "Yum," Sheila muttered.

The video also described a study from about ten years ago, which found that as the glue, paper, and ink on paper start to biodegrade, they emit pleasing compounds. But the video didn't say anything about studies of pheromones in the books. Sheila hoped this was because no one had thought of it before. Maybe she *could* get her PhD with this kind of idea.

Next, Sheila searched the websites of the three local universities to see if they had botany departments. Only one did, and it offered a PhD in plant and microbial biology. She peered at the staff list. The head of the department was Dr. Peter Gordon. His photo was not what she expected. No bow tie. No facial wrinkles. His tousled curly brown hair framed kind eyes behind round wire-rimmed glasses. He wore a brown T-shirt, which made him seem approachable and earthy—not like a stuffy academic.

The description beneath his photo said: "Research in my lab focuses on understanding how biological interactions and the environment affect plant evolution and behavior. We use a variety of molecular approaches—population genetics, greenhouse and field studies, and quantitative genetics—in this quest. I am currently involved in a variety of projects investigating the ecological and evolutionary limits to species range expansion and how different species of plants interact. I also remain interested in understanding the interaction between plants, animals, and humans."

A little thrill ran through Sheila. She was distracted the rest of the day, thinking about Professor Gordon's research.

As she worked, she formulated a plan. But before she could implement it, she needed another foggy day to see if she could replicate her experience with Cubby and the tree. She'd be more confident in her plan if something similar happened again.

A WEEK AND A HALF LATER, Sheila awoke to a foggy Saturday morning. Even though she usually walked Cubby at noon, she decided on an early walk before the mist had a chance to burn off. Sheila shoved a cap over her bed-head hair and made sure to turn on Cubby's tracking device and clip it to his collar. She slipped her phone into her pocket as they headed out the door.

Walking down the street, Sheila remembered her promise to let Jason help. But wasn't 7 a.m. too early to bug him, especially on a Saturday? She hoped he would understand.

The scent of the neighbor's lilac bush enveloped her. Sheila inhaled deeply as they passed, enjoying this smell of spring. Juneberry bushes sported white flowers at the entrance to the trail. The blossoms would soon change into navy blue berries, perfect for jam and sauce. Fog lingered but thinned as they entered the woods.

After a few steps, Sheila stopped. Reaching the end of his leash, Cubby looked back at her, questioning. She wondered if she was ready for this experiment. An ancient part of her, rooted in prehistory and connected to the Earth, recognized the wisdom of her apprehension. Another part of her felt foolish for expecting anything to happen.

Well, it's now or never. She unhooked Cubby's leash. He trotted ahead, sniffing young trees near the trail. She wondered if the fog portended a hot, muggy day. She could smell the dirt and the growth of everything green. The leaves on the trees were full-grown now, providing a dense canopy that heightened the gloom.

Sheila stopped to inhale and slowly spun around on the trail, her arms outstretched. Tendrils of fog twisted and slowly twirled around her, spinning off in eddies as if she were underwater.

The logical part of her brain intruded, instructing her to keep an eye on Cubby. She stopped and peered ahead. The small rise was ahead. She couldn't see Cubby and assumed he must have already passed over it.

Sheila strode up the small hill. She stopped on top, scanning for Cubby. A jolt of adrenaline shot through her—he was nowhere in sight. Worried, she jogged down the other side, peering as far as she could into the thick woods. She still couldn't see him. She halted just past the leek bed, where Cubby had gone missing before. "Cubby! Here, boy!"

Nothing. Then she remembered her phone. She took it out. As she waited for the GPS app to load, she called Cubby, straining to hear his footsteps.

Still nothing.

Sheila stared at the phone screen. Where was the little blue pinging signal? In desperation, she held her phone higher as if that might help catch the signal. *Damn.* Where was that dog? Was the fog blocking the signal?

She called Cubby. Only the muted chirping of birds replied.

Here we go again. She walked over to the same large tree she had hugged. It stood straight, immutable, mysterious. She laid her cheek against the rough damp bark and encircled the trunk with her arms.

Please bring my dog back to me. Please . . .

She waited a few heartbeats. No sound of doggy footsteps through the leaves resulted from her plea this time. Sheila closed her eyes and tried again, hugging the tree harder.

Nothing.

She stepped back and called to Cubby again. The only answers were the distant rustling of squirrels. Deeper and deeper into the gloom she went, calling.

Sheila decided to check the other side of the trail. She made her way back, looking left and right. Standing on the trail, she shouted into the woods. She walked into the forest.

After twenty minutes of fruitless searching on the other side of the trail, Sheila trudged back to it, disheartened. She tried the GPS again, unsuccessfully. She checked her watch. It was almost 8:00. Maybe it was still too early to call her friends, but texting might be okay. She texted Tina first and then Jason, asking them for their help searching for Cubby.

While she waited for a response, she walked home and got into her car. She drove around the neighborhood, looking for Cubby in case he came out of the forest and onto the road.

A tan-reddish shape burst from the woods and ran out onto the road. Her heart caught, but it was just a deer.

Her cell rang and Sheila pulled over. The screen said it was Tina. Tina didn't waste time with hello. "Have you found him yet?"

"No. Now I'm driving around, looking."

"Oh, Sheila, you sound upset."

"No kidding. I thought I found him, but it was a deer."

"And the GPS doesn't work?"

"No. I don't see anything on the screen. I don't understand it."

"Do you still want me to come help find him?"

"Could you?" Sheila asked.

"No problem. Give me fifteen minutes and I'll be there."

"Thanks, Tina. You're a gem. Meet me at my house."

Next, Jason called. He was as mystified as Sheila about why the GPS wasn't working. He said he'd come help look for Cubby, too.

Sheila clicked off her phone and pulled back out onto the road, heading home. She parked her car in the garage and waited on the back steps for her friends. She checked the phone app again. Still no sign of her dog. She opened the "about" section of the app to see if there were any clues about why it wasn't working. As she read, she came across a sentence about how dense tree cover can interfere with the accuracy of the app. *Oh, great,* she thought. *It doesn't work in the forest—the one place where I need it!* But maybe it would help her locate Cubby if he came out of the woods.

Tina and Jason arrived at about the same time. As they all walked toward the trail, Jason said, "Don't kill me for asking, but are you sure you turned the tracker on?"

Sheila gave him a look, eyes narrowed.

Jason held up his hands, "Okay, okay!"

They searched on the side of the trail where Cubby originally went missing, working in a grid pattern. She paced the middle grid with each of her friends on either side of her about twenty feet away.

They walked through the forest, calling Cubby's name. The longer they went without finding him, the heavier Sheila's heart became. Cubby had been her constant companion since she moved into her aunt's house. He cuddled with her while they watched television, leaning his eighty pounds against her. He was first to greet her in the morning, and the last being she saw at night. Her throat tightened at the thought of the huge empty space he would leave in her life if they didn't find him. A maraschino cherry of guilt topped it all off. She felt responsible for losing him—she just *had* to do this crazy tree experiment, didn't she?

By now, the searchers had moved deep into the forest. The fog still lay as thick as before. Sheila's jeans were soaked from brushing through the ferns and thimbleberry bushes. They'd been searching for about a half hour when Sheila noticed a dark shape in the corner of her eye, off to her right.

The misty gray form was about the size of a person. It hovered several feet off the ground. Afraid to make a sudden movement, Sheila slowly turned her head to see better. At the top of the shape, filaments of denser fog spread out from what seemed like a head.

Sheila stood still, not believing what she saw. She closed her eyes and opened them again. The shape was still there. It appeared to be an old woman with long, white hair. Sheila's breath caught. She could hear Tina and Jason calling for Cubby on either side of her. She feared the shadowy form would disperse if she made any loud sound. She whispered, "Aunt Miranda?"

The being turned toward her. Its luminous blue eyes gazed into hers. The hairs on Sheila's arms prickled as they rose. No mistaking it—those eyes were exactly like her aunt's.

The ghostly woman raised her arm and pointed deeper into the fog.

"Thank you," Sheila whispered. As she headed in the direction the apparition indicated, she called to Tina and Jason. "Hey guys, follow me!"

Her aunt vanished, replaced by a swirling gray wall.

"What is it?" Tina called, crashing through the brush.

"Not sure. Just follow me!" Sheila could hear Jason running from her other side. She kept walking, not wanting to miss whatever her aunt had pointed toward. After a few moments, she entered a grove of white pines she'd never seen before. The trees loomed above her, primeval and weathered, their branches covered with green feathery needles.

In the middle of the grove stood a huge pine, a monarch of the forest. Sheila estimated it would take more than five people holding hands, arms outstretched, to encircle it. Burn marks marred the trunk, reaching about five feet up the side. The lowest branches began at least twenty feet up and were thick around as her waist. Shelia looked up . . . and up . . . and up and couldn't see the top. Was this what her aunt had been pointing at?

Sheila could hear Tina shuffling through the underbrush behind her, and then Jason. *Woah* was their collective reaction. Sheila turned and glanced over her shoulder, putting one hand out in a "stay there" gesture. She slowly walked around the right side of the tree. Pearl-sized drops of sap sparkled in the crevices of its thick bark. The burn scar formed a dark cavity. After a few more steps, she stopped, blinking her eyes in disbelief. Cubby sat inside the alcove. He faced her, panting, wearing a doggy smile as if this were all good fun.

"Cubby!" she cried, rushing forward. The dog remained sitting and let Sheila rub his furry ears. He peered into her eyes with devotion and trust, as if apologizing for worrying her. "C'mon, Cubby, let's get you out of there." Sheila tugged on his collar. He took a few steps, then stopped. "What? What's up?"

Tina had followed Sheila around the tree. "It looks like he doesn't want to leave," she said.

Sheila stood in front of the tree, her mind racing. Cubby sat and wouldn't budge. She did the only thing that seemed to make sense: she clambered into the hollow with him. As soon as she did, something knocked her on her butt. Sheila sat down hard with an "Ooof!"

Jason had joined Tina, and they stepped forward. They bent over, hands on their knees, mouths moving.

Sheila couldn't hear them. She did hear Cubby's panting, though. As she petted him, a frizz of electricity enveloped her, as if her dog were attached to an electric fence. At first, she thought the low shock must be hurting Cubby, but he just sat, unchanged, tongue lolling as goofily as usual.

Now Tina and Jason were gesticulating. Watching them was tiring. What were they so worried about? She was right here, with her dog. Sheila's eyelids grew heavy, so she closed them. She put an arm out to steady herself, touching the inside of the tree. The electric sensation intensified, but not enough to make her uncomfortable.

A flood of images ran through her. Her viewpoint was up high, as if from a treetop. She could see herself and Aunt Miranda walking the trail as they had done a couple of years ago, shuffling through the red and yellow leaves. Her aunt remarked that the trees did not produce acorns that year. Not one tree—as if all of them had one mind. Aunt Miranda had wondered aloud if the weather just wasn't right that year. Sheila hadn't known what to think.

The old white pine slowly sent Sheila a concept, luminous and simple: *PROTEST.*

Of course! It all became so clear. The trees wanted people to notice them—to notice the change. By withholding their acorns, their young, they were protesting what humans were doing to their home: pollution, climate change, development . . . all the things people were so good at but were so harmful to life. Her aunt must have been right: they *did* have one mind.

"I hear you. I understand," she whispered.

That image faded only to open on a pile of dead trees and brush. Sheila recognized it from the bulldozing done a couple of blocks away near the neighborhood shopping center. Logs lay scattered across the barren landscape like bones from a wolf kill. The landowners claimed they were taking care of overdue landscaping, but Sheila and most of her neighbors knew they were making way for more development—either an addition to the strip mall or an apartment building to match the one that just went in at the intersection nearby.

Along with a whiff of fresh pine scent, another thought floated behind her eyes: *ENOUGH.*

She said, "I hear you. I understand."

A sharp pain lanced through her head. Sheila opened her eyes to see Jason trying to reach inside the cavity's opening. He yanked his hand back as if burned, cradling it between his legs. She shook her head vigorously. He slowly stood and backed away. She closed her eyes again. The tree had more to say.

An image of her church, about half a mile away, appeared. Her congregation prided itself on its "green" tendencies. She could make out the scraggly plants growing on the church's green roof and the birch tree designs that decorated its front windows.

Three men with chainsaws walked through the apron of land between the parking lot in front of the church and the road that paralleled it. A few aspens were leaning over, bowed by high winter winds. The trees inclined on their upright neighbors like tired soldiers. They weren't in imminent danger of falling or doing any damage to cars in the lot or on the road, they were just crooked. Nevertheless, the men began sawing away at them.

Sheila could hear the aspens' piercing shrieks—like a thousand buzzing cicadas—as the teeth of the chainsaws sliced into their bark. She covered her ears with her hands, her eyes still closed. The shrieking rose in intensity until, mercifully, the scene started to fade along with the sounds.

Another word floated into her thoughts: *HELP.*

Trees could feel? Trees could scream? Nothing in her life had prepared Sheila for this. Images passed of all the times she had broken a twig off a tree in passing as she hiked, helped her father chop wood in the backyard of her childhood home, or watched neighbors cut down old trees that had become safety hazards. Nausea rose within her. She took her hands from her ears and put them over her mouth.

Cubby's body pressed against her. Sheila rocked back and forth, feeling constricted by the tree cavity, too shocked and ill from the information the tree provided.

Not daring to remove her hands from her mouth and speak, Sheila sent a thought to the tree: *I hear you. I understand.*

She opened her eyes. Cubby's worried gaze bored into hers. She grabbed him, started to rise, pulled him through the opening with her. She expected a sharp shock or some kind of webby resistance. Nothing stopped them.

Sheila stood, gasping for breath, feeling free. The nausea was still with her, though. She stumbled a few steps and spewed her sickness onto the forest floor. Cubby followed and sat next to her as she stood, wiping her mouth with the back of her hand. Soon, she felt a touch on her shoulder. She turned to see Tina with Jason close behind.

"Are you okay?" Tina's brow furrowed.

"Yes . . . no. Oh, man, that was . . ." Sheila glanced at the old pine, standing so still. The fire scar silent and innocent, as if nothing had happened. "C'mon, let's get out of here." She took the leash from her pocket and hooked it onto Cubby.

"I'm not going to argue with that," Jason said, falling in line with the women.

Shell-shocked, they walked out of the woods. The fog had burned off, and the day was warming with a spring mugginess. Sheila kept looking behind as if expecting a follower. At the house, she invited her friends inside for lunch. She wasn't sure she could eat, but she could at least be hospitable.

Once inside, she turned her attention to Jason's hand. He held it out to her. An angry red welt splashed across his palm and partway onto the back of it. She ran cold water in the sink. As she submerged his hand, she said, "It's probably not burning any more, but this could help if it is."

"It feels good. Thanks." Jason gave her a slight smile.

After a few minutes, he took his hand out of the water and Sheila gently toweled it off. The act felt uncomfortably intimate. It was bad enough he was even in her house. She took a tube of ointment from the medicine cabinet. "Here. Put this on. There's some gauze and tape in the cabinet."

"Got it," Jason said.

Reentering the kitchen, she saw Tina rubbing Cubby's ears. "He seems just fine," she said.

"Well, that makes one of us." Sheila chuckled.

She would warm up some tomato soup. As she stood at the stove, her hand shook as she stirred the soup pot.

Tina asked if she could help. Sheila told her where to find the ingredients for grilled cheese sandwiches. As Sheila placed the electric griddle on the counter, Tina asked, "What *was* that? What happened to you in the tree?"

Sheila plugged in the griddle, shaking her head. "I don't know. I can't talk about it and cook at the same time." She took her hand off the cord and masked its shaking by smoothing it on her pants. "Let's wait till we eat, okay?"

Tina nodded. Cubby ran down the hall to greet Jason as he came out of the bathroom. The dog led him back into the kitchen like a grand marshal in a parade.

"We just need to finish the sandwiches. Almost ready," Sheila said, ladling the soup into bowls.

"Smells good." Jason sat at the kitchen table, cradling his bandaged hand.

As Cubby curled up in his favorite spot on the couch, the trio ate in silence. Sheila's nausea had disappeared, and she found it easier to eat than she expected.

Tina broached the subject again, "What was it like, in the tree?"

Sheila looked hard at her companions, especially at Jason. "I can trust you guys, right? Like, you won't have me committed for anything I'm about to say?"

Tina and Jason swore to keep her secrets.

Sheila asked, "Did you see anything on the way to the tree—like a figure of a person or anything?" Her friends shook their heads. This both relieved Sheila and worried her. Had she just imagined seeing her aunt? Then again, Aunt Miranda had probably disappeared before Tina and Jason arrived.

"Okay, well, I got into the tree, and it was like this force was keeping me there—an electric buzzy force. It showed me images."

"Of what?" Jason asked.

Sheila hesitated. "Of what it's like to be a tree." Now both of Sheila's hands started shaking. She clasped them between her knees under the table. "The tree told me three things. Very clear words: protest, enough, and help."

"That's crazy," Jason said.

Tina gave him a sharp glance, saying, "You promised!"

"Okay, okay." He drew his unbandaged hand through his hair. "I'm just a little freaked out—this whole thing."

Sheila put one of her hands back on the table. It was steadier now. "I know this is weird, but you have to believe me—the tree communicated with me. It was like the tree used Cubby as a lure to get me into the burn scar so it could talk to me." Staring at Jason, she said, "If you don't believe it, you can leave right now. If it's too much for you, go!"

Jason looked sheepish. "Well, I haven't finished lunch yet."

"OMG, men! Always thinking of their stomachs." Tina laughed. Then she glanced at Sheila. "Sorry, Sheila. I know this is serious."

Sheila sighed and took a sip of her soup, collecting her thoughts and her nerve. She told them about the images that accompanied each of the tree's words. "The trees need our help. They've let me know they can think and feel and act. They are sentient, like us, but different. We need—" Sheila hesitated, "*I* need to let people know we're hurting them. The things we do affect them."

"I admit something happened to you inside that tree," Jason said. "I mean, I felt the force or whatever it was that was keeping you in there, it even burned me, but a tree communicating? That's a hard one." He took a bite of his sandwich.

"Well, how would you explain it?" Sheila asked.

Jason chewed some more, his forehead furrowed. "I admit, I can't."

Tina watched them like she was at a slow-motion tennis match.

"I don't know why the tree lured me. You're the one it should have targeted. You're the one that needs convincing," Sheila said.

Tina interjected, "Well, you're the one the trees know. You walk that trail all the time. Maybe . . . maybe they know they can trust you. Maybe they know you're open to what they have to say."

"Well, I'm just glad that everyone's okay and that we found Cubby," Jason said. "Hey, thanks for the lunch. I gotta go run some errands." He rose from the table and put his dishes in the sink. "You ladies have a good day. I'll see you on Monday."

Tina looked at Sheila as if gauging her reaction. Sheila knew nothing else she could say would bring him around. It might even hinder his understanding. Maybe he needed to come to the realization himself. Pushing too hard would drive him away.

Sheila went to the back door to let him out. "Thanks so much for your help today, Jason. I really appreciate it."

Back inside, Sheila and Tina continued eating. Tina dipped her sandwich into her soup. "What do you think is going on with him?"

"I don't know. I don't know him well enough." Sheila turned on the radio that sat near the wall on the kitchen table. Music from the local college station filled the kitchen.

"Do you remember that time we took those boys from our school through the storm sewer on Hillcrest Drive?"

Tina's question transported Sheila back to her childhood neighborhood on the other side of town. She could almost feel the lumpy asphalt beneath her feet as she and Tina walked with the two boys in tow. John and Dan were visiting their neighborhood for the first time, lured by the prospect of spending time with two sixteen-year-old girls. Crawling through the storm sewers was a neighborhood initiation rite Sheila had created not long before.

As they walked down a hill toward a ravine, the boys had exchanged nervous glances. Capitalizing on their feelings, Tina said, "It's fun. We haven't lost anyone yet. Don't worry."

"We aren't worried, are we, Dan?" said John, the swarthier of the two. He had long brown hair and a bad-boy strut.

Dan was a dishwater blond who moved with less self-assurance. "Count me in," he said.

The four teenagers reached the ravine and followed Sheila down the bank to the opening of a large cement stormwater culvert. It looked roomy enough for them to fit into if they bent at the waist. A trickle of water flowed inside, disappearing in the direction they would be traveling—that is, if the boys didn't back out.

They sat in the gravel on the banks of the leafy ravine. Sheila gazed at John and Dan, sizing them up. "Okay, you guys follow us. Don't stop. If you feel like you're going to freak out, say something." Sheila paused for a moment. "You aren't claustrophobic, are you?"

The boys shook their heads.

"All right. This doesn't take long, and it's sort of fun to see the underbelly of our 'hood. You ready?"

"Lead on, girls," John said. "Adventure awaits."

They entered the culvert, Sheila leading with Tina next. The boys followed. The cool air in the culvert smelled of musty green water and concrete dust. The light quickly dimmed as they made their way inside.

Sheila walked with her feet straddling the water, not wanting to get her tennies wet. They were all quiet, concentrating on making their way through the subterranean recesses.

Soon, they reached a junction where three culverts joined. The girls stopped. "You can stand," Tina said to the boys. Her voice echoed off the walls and the higher ceiling. They stood, sighing in relief. Dim light filtered through the manhole cover overhead.

"Which way do we go?" John asked.

"You trust us? You *really* trust us?" Sheila asked.

The boys looked at each other and shrugged. "What choice do we have?" asked Dan.

"Smart!" said Sheila. "This way." She took a left and followed that culvert, straddling the small stream of water as before. The light dimmed again as they traveled deeper into the system.

Sheila stopped abruptly, and everyone piled into her.

"Ow! What's wrong?" asked John.

"Umm, I think I might have taken a wrong turn." Sheila's voice quavered.

"What—you mean we're lost?"

"No, it just means we need to turn around," Tina said.

Sheila could hear the boys scuffling and then crawling back the way they came. After a few moments, she called, "Just kidding! We're going the right way."

The boys grumbled, but they started to shuffle back. The girls giggled. After about thirty feet, the culvert started to brighten.

"Almost there," Tina said.

The boys didn't respond, but Sheila could still hear their footfalls behind. After another dozen feet, she could see the end of the culvert. As she jumped out of the opening, she said, "Welcome to the neighborhood, gentlemen!"

The boys stepped out, squinting into the shade-dappled sun. Trees surrounded the ravine, which continued down the hill. Sheila and Tina had followed the watercourse a few times and knew that the storm drain runoff eventually joined a local creek that flowed down the hillside and into the harbor.

Sheila sat, and the rest joined her on a grassy spot on the bank. Dan sat next to Sheila and John next to Tina. A willow tree loomed above, sheltering them with its drooping branches.

"That wasn't so bad," Dan said. "You ever have anyone who freaked out?"

"Nope." Sheila brushed a strand of hair away from her face, suddenly self-conscious. "Been lucky, I guess. But we haven't done it all that much. Not too many new people move here." They sat for a while in companionable silence. "Don't tell anyone we did this, though. We might get in trouble."

"I solemnly swear." Dan crossed his chest. "Hey, what are you going to do after high school?"

The change in topics surprised Sheila. "Uh, I dunno. My parents want me to stay here and go to college. That's probably what I'll do."

"Do you know what you're going to study?"

"Library science. I like books. It just seems like the thing to do," Sheila said. "What are you going to do?"

"Maybe join the Navy. I'd love to see the ocean." Dan got a wistful look in his eyes. Sheila envied his world view. In comparison, her options seemed so limited. She often got the feeling her parents didn't want her to leave town and leave them. She was their only child. Her father, Ralph, owned a dry-cleaning business and her mother, Nancy, stayed at home. Theirs was a firmly middle-class existence. Maybe even lower middle-class.

As Sheila studied Dan, she caught sight of John and Tina. John had one hand to Tina's face. It seemed like he was going to kiss her. She knew Tina had never been kissed. Not wanting to interrupt the moment for her friend, Sheila tore her gaze away and focused on Dan. Did he want to kiss her? Talking with him was nice, but she wasn't sure she wanted more.

When the group rose to leave for Tina's house a few minutes later, John and Tina's faces were flushed.

Back in her kitchen in the present, Sheila swallowed a spoonful of soup. "I remember you got your first kiss that day."

"I always felt bad we gave those guys such a hard time," Tina said. "What do you think ever happened to them?"

"I wouldn't be surprised if John spent some time in prison. Dan was nice, but sort of . . . meh."

"What do you think of Jason?" Tina asked.

"You like him?"

Tina finished the last bit of her sandwich. She looked Sheila square in the eyes. "Yeah, he seems cool."

"More power to you, sista. He's handsome, but I make it a rule not to date anyone who doesn't believe trees can communicate." They laughed. "Our little escapade this morning probably scared him away for good, anyway."

"Could be. I guess we'll be able to tell when we see him at work," Tina said.

While they were musing, the song "Stranded" played on the radio. "Oh, I love this song," Tina said. "Turn it up!" The musician was Samuel "Corn Boy" Collins from Minneapolis.

Oh baby, why'd you sail away and leave me, stranded on this shore? Baby, oh baby why don't you say you love me anymore?

The song made Sheila wish she had someone to love as much as Sam loved the woman who inspired his song. "Didn't he write that about his fiancée?" she asked Tina.

"Oh yeah." A dreamy glaze crossed Tina's face. "They got married last year. It's so romantic. She lived in the apartment next to his and he used to hear her singing in the shower. Something she sang inspired this song. Then she disappeared 'cause she was quarantined. And he searched for her and found her!" Tina was all smiles.

"Hmph," was all Sheila said.

"You're only twenty-six—too young to be so jaded."

"If you're interested in Jason, go for it," Sheila said. "Seriously, I don't think he and I would get along as well as you two could."

Tina just grinned.

A FEW DAYS LATER, Sheila phoned Professor Gordon during work. He answered, his voice resonant and friendly. Sheila took care not to say her name, only that she was a freelance writer working on a story about communication among plants.

"I saw on the university website that you're interested in understanding the interaction between plants, animals, and humans. I thought you might be a good resource for my story."

After a pause, the professor said, "I mostly investigate how animals and humans depend on plants as resources, but . . . I'm intrigued by recent research that shows how plants communicate with each other and the influences they can have on other species, as well."

"Have you done any research into plant communication?"

"It's hard to find funding for that, but I've been doing a few projects on my own time. Ever hear of the Bagley Nature Area?"

"Oh yeah, it's not far from my house." Sheila tried to hide her honest enthusiasm. The nature area was adjacent to the college and only about a mile away from her home.

"I've got some research plots set up there. I've had a few intriguing results."

"Would you be willing to discuss them with me?" Sheila said.

Professor Gordon agreed, and they set up a time to meet. She thanked him for his time. "My pleasure," he said. "I'm always willing to help." Sheila disconnected the call and sat back in her chair, smiling.

Down a few rows of bookcases, she could see Jason shelving. His back was toward her, and she scrutinized his burned hand. It was unbandaged with only a slight red mark. She got up and went over to him.

"Your hand is looking better. How's it feel?" she asked.

Jason considered, flexing his hand. "It feels good," he said. "Almost all better." He finished shelving the book he was holding. Then he turned to her. "Hey, I'm sorry about how I acted at your place last weekend."

Sheila was about to say something nice—something to let him off the hook, but he continued, "I was a little freaked out. I mean . . . stuff like that doesn't happen every day. I still don't know what to make of it all. But I'm glad you're okay and that Cubby's okay."

"Thanks," Sheila said. "I was really glad for your help, and Tina's. I'm still sort of processing it all myself. But . . . we're cool, right? You, me, Tina?"

"Yeah," Jason said. "We're cool. A little weird, but cool."

ON A BRIGHT DAY with a warm breeze, Sheila's nerves rattled as she drove to the college to meet Professor Gordon. She didn't want him to know her name or where she worked because she wasn't exactly dealing with things that were strictly scientific. She wasn't sure how he would react to her line of questioning. Still, she wasn't comfortable misrepresenting herself. She considered coming clean as soon as they met, but then discarded the idea. She'd wait and see what impressions she received from him about the whole trees communicating thing. If he thought she was loony, she'd at least have some measure of privacy.

Sheila parked her car in the large lot reserved for the public and made her way through the maze of connected buildings to the Botany Department. Professor Gordon's gray door was ajar a few inches. She knocked.

His voice, deep and resonant, vibrated, "Hold on . . . be right there."

As Sheila waited, she read a newspaper story tacked to a bulletin board in the hall about a perfectly preserved bog boy that was found in Meadowlands, a small town not far away. Before she could finish the story, she heard Professor Gordon finishing a phone call. ". . . Fine, Randall. That's a great idea for a project. I'll be in touch."

Then he was standing in front of her in faded jeans and with tousled hair. His green eyes surprised and delighted her. Their color hadn't come through in the departmental photo she'd seen. Also missing from the photo were the tattoos snaking down his forearms from under his T-shirt.

"Come in," he said, gesturing to a chair near his desk.

She walked in and sat down, clasping her hands in her lap to keep from fidgeting. She thanked him for meeting with her then she stared blankly. Although she had recited her opening lines in her bedroom, the words seemed to have fled from her like mischievous children. Finally, she stammered, "Professor Gordon, I know you're busy, so I'll get to the point. I'm interested in your research into plant communication. Your initial journal articles on the topic are intriguing. Are you working on anything similar now?"

Professor Gordon sat back and steepled his hands under his chin. "Well, as I mentioned on the phone, I've got a plot in the Bagley Nature Area where I'm investigating the underground connections between the older-growth trees and young trees. This vast network of fungi exists that connects the older trees—the grandfather and grandmother trees, if you will—to the younger trees. They share information that way. Information, and some think, even nutrients. The older, more established trees can help the younger ones survive that way."

"Doesn't that go against the whole 'survival of the fittest' concept?" Sheila asked.

"Yes and no. It goes against the theory if you think of trees as individuals. It aligns with the theory if you think of a certain species of trees as a colony versus other plants or tree species. Some researchers think groves of trees are acting as a single unit."

Sheila pushed him a little. "And what do you think?"

Professor Gordon regarded her. "Well, if we're going to get into opinions on this topic, you might as well call me

Peter." He smiled slightly. "By the way, I don't think I caught your name."

The question caught Sheila off guard. After a few beats, she said, "My name's Sheila. Nice to meet you." She hoped she wouldn't regret revealing this much of her identity later.

Peter's smile widened. "Well, I think there are many, many things we don't understand about how trees communicate with each other or with other species."

As Sheila's nerves quieted, she noticed the tattoos on Peter's arms featured twisting fern and palm fronds. Was it her imagination, or were there more leaves than when she first saw them? A nameless, magnetic force pulled her toward this man, unlike anything she had experienced. She fought to push it aside as she formulated her next question.

"What about tree-to-human communication?" she asked.

"What do you have in mind?"

Sheila had come this far, she might as well go the whole way. She blurted, "I have this theory that the chemicals from trees that are in paper can influence human moods."

Peter leaned forward as if encouraging her to continue.

"Have you ever opened a book and had that *smell* waft up into your nose? It makes you feel good, right?"

Peter nodded.

"What if it's more than just the book scent." She hesitated. Her heart was hammering. "What if it's from the chemicals in the wood? What if, even in their deaths, trees can influence us once they've been made into books?"

Peter peered at the ceiling for a moment. "That would be a complicated study but doable." He looked back to Sheila. "It would just take a control group—say, people exposed to paper made from something other than trees—and then a group of people exposed to regular paper. It would have to be double-blind, of course . . ."

Sheila watched as Peter's mind worked. Gradually, she relaxed. He didn't seem to care that she wasn't a writer. It was all about the ideas.

"Finding funding might be difficult, but maybe one of the local paper companies would be willing. If you're right, it could be a big boost to their industry." Peter leaned forward and Sheila could almost see a cog clicking into place inside him. It seemed like a good cog, a helpful, unbiased cog.

"How far along are you with your story?" he asked.

"I'm sorry, Professor Gordon . . . Peter. I'm not actually a writer. I'm a reference librarian who's had some interesting experiences with trees. I guess I just needed someone to talk to about it." Sheila sighed and looked down to the floor, awaiting his judgement.

"I thought it might be something like that." Peter studied her face. "Why did you feel you needed to tell me you were a writer?"

Sheila looked him square in the eye. "You've got to admit plant communication is kind of *out there*. I needed to feel you out, first."

Peter was silent for a moment. "I guess I don't blame you. I feel some of those same pressures at times with my colleagues."

Then, it was as if a reset switch had been reprogrammed between them because Peter continued, "You know what, I could use a mind like yours on my team. I've got a job posted for a research assistant. You don't have to be enrolled to apply, but it would give you an advantage if you were." He picked up an open notebook from his desk and handed it to Sheila along with a pen. His warm hand touched hers, briefly. "If you give me your email address, I'll send you the listing."

Sheila wrote her personal email address. She had told this man a white lie, and now he was offering her a job? As she handed the notebook back, she said, "I appreciate your understanding. I'll take a look at the job. It sounds interesting."

"You should come see my plot, too. If you get the job, you'll be spending a lot of time there."

"Oh, I'd like to see that either way," Sheila said. They agreed to meet next week, weather permitting.

As she walked back to her car, excitement welled up in her along with chagrin. Peter hadn't laughed out loud at her theory. It didn't hurt that he was good-looking, either. She wondered if he was married. She was so distracted by his tattoos that she forgot to look at his ring finger.

A WEEK LATER, SHEILA AND PETER met in a parking lot near the nature area. Spring had begun giving way to summer. Lush greenery enveloped them as they started walking. The trail started at a pond, following its edge. Shortly, it turned into the woods. The path narrowed from a yard-wide grassy swath to a dirt track through maples and oaks.

Peter walked with long, sure strides but Sheila had no trouble keeping up. He asked if she had a chance to read the job posting. Sheila groaned. She knew this question would be coming but wasn't ready to commit to applying yet.

"Yes, thanks for sending it to me," she said. "I plan on applying, but I'm worried. I like my job at the library and this job you're offering is so different from anything else I've ever done."

Peter looked thoughtful. "I suppose it is different from being a librarian. But you do research for that, don't you?"

Sheila hesitated. "Yes . . . but I learn things from books. I don't do primary research in a specific field. That's a whole different animal."

"I think you'll find it's not all that different. It's just a bit more direct perhaps. Of course, I can't force you to apply, but I would encourage it. I suspect you'd do well in the job, just from what little I know of you.

"One of the perks of being a university employee is that you can take classes for free. This may be getting way ahead of things, but if you like the work and want to pursue a graduate degree, you could do it just for the cost of books."

Before Sheila could think of what to say next, they topped a rise. Ahead lay a large fenced-in area of forest.

"Here we are. Research Area 16-N," Peter said.

"Why is it named that?" Sheila asked. "Did you mess up fifteen other plots?"

Peter laughed. "No. I just finished fencing it on the sixteenth of last November, just before the ground totally froze. I decided that was as good a namesake as any."

Sheila crinkled her nose. "Well, it sounds impressive, anyway."

"I'll tell you a secret, though," Peter said. Then he whispered, "In my mind, I call it Birch Grove."

Sheila smiled. "I like that name much better."

He led her along the side of the fence, bushwhacking through brush and small trees. "I didn't want to put the gate too close to the trail," he explained. "This way, people are less likely to find it and mess around in here." He stopped and worked the crude latch, holding the gate so that Sheila could enter first.

As he worked on fastening the gate, Sheila looked around. The plot seemed a mishmash of many tree species: birch, spruce, white pines, and maples, but birch predominated. A few large trees were scattered among many younger ones. "What type of forest is this, anyway?" she asked.

Peter walked a few steps into the enclosure. "It's a transition zone between a maple-oak forest and a boreal ecosystem. I chose it for the variety of species and the mixture of ages." He held onto a spindly tree. "There's young ones, like this birch here, and big old ones, like that white pine." He pointed farther into the enclosure to a tree that looked like it could easily be a hundred years old.

"Cool," Sheila said.

"Here, let me show you something." They walked several yards farther in and stopped near a large birch. Peter turned to face her, and then looked up to the top of the tree. As his gaze returned to her, he began. "Especially in the forest, looks can be deceiving. We think of trees as stationary, mute, powerless against natural forces. They seem to just stand here and grow. Some might get cut down, some fall and that's it. Simple, right?"

Sheila thought, *You have no idea*, and nodded, playing along.

"But in reality, the forest is incredibly complicated. Some trees shade out others. Nurse logs help young trees grow, giving them nutrients and shelter. While it's true trees don't move, they can send out their pollen across the forest, they can communicate with other trees through pheromones in the air and through fungus underground. They produce mild toxins to keep insects at bay, produce nuts to lure animals to spread their seeds across the forest. The forest ecosystem is dynamic and complex . . ." His gaze lingered on her face.

Sheila blushed and looked down. As she did, her gaze sought his left hand. No ring! A frisson of hope bloomed inside her.

"I've got several experiments going on here." Peter leaned his ringless hand on the birch. "The first examines how some trees help others. This birch here is one of the helper trees— like a grandmother or grandfather tree, if you will."

Sheila tore her gaze away from his hand and inspected the tree more closely. She noticed tiny white bags on the ends of some of the branches, and a few wires and instruments taped to the trunk higher up.

Peter walked her around the tree, explaining what the various devices measured. "In essence, this tree is looking out for the other trees, above ground and below." He took a small trowel from his pocket, crouched, and began digging. As he worked, the tattoos on his arm seemed to writhe slightly. When his trough reached about five inches deep, he sat back and beckoned for Sheila to come closer. He pointed at some white filaments. His professorial tone was replaced by a boyish enthusiasm. "See these? Magnificent! This is part of the communication network between this birch," then he nodded his head at a small pine near Sheila, "and that balsam fir."

Sheila liked his fervor. "How do you know?"

"A researcher in Canada proved it, and I'm replicating her work—testing to see if what's happening in her woods is happening here. We cover the young birches and balsams with bags and expose one of the trees to a gas with a radioactive tracer in it. The tracer travels through the root system and the fungus filaments. Then we test the other trees to see which ones receive the tracer. That way, we know which trees are communicating with each other. Of course, I'll test the other nearby tree species, too, but the Canadian studies showed that only birch and fir seem to have this link." Peter peered up at her, his eyes twinkling behind his glasses.

"Wow, that's really cool. I had no idea!" Sheila paused to think. "Well, I had somewhat of an idea because I've read *The Overstory*, but I didn't know it was happening here. Do we know why it's these two species that work together?"

Peter gave a lighthearted laugh. "No, we're at the very beginning stages of our understanding—at the kindergarten level. But if you can stand going back to your childhood, so to speak, this would be the job for you." He set to work again, covering up the trough in the ground with the excess dirt he'd piled beside it.

"I'd love to read a copy of the Canadian researcher's paper."

"I'll email it to you." Peter straightened and led the way out of the enclosure, securing the gate behind them.

As they bushwhacked back to the trail, Sheila marveled at Peter's enthusiasm for his research. Maybe she could tell him about her experience with Cubby and the giant white pine.

It was as if Peter could read her mind. When they reached the trail, he asked, "So, you said you'd had some interesting experiences with trees. Would you mind sharing what they were?" He glanced over his shoulder at Sheila. She looked down, thoughts racing. Was she reading him correctly? Could she tell Peter without him laughing in her face?

She decided she could. "I live near Wickham Park, and I take my dog walking there almost every day."

"Oh, what breed of dog?"

"A goldendoodle. His name is Cubby."

"I love dogs. Sorry, please continue."

"I took Cubby out walking one foggy Saturday morning and he disappeared, which is unlike him. He did it once before but came back not long after. This last time, he didn't come back, no matter how long I called for him. I searched all over and couldn't find him. Finally, I called a couple of my friends, and they helped me look." Sheila remembered the ghostly form of her aunt pointing the way in the forest. She was already pushing things, telling Peter about the huge white pine. It was probably better to leave her aunt's ghost out of it.

She continued, "We found Cubby far off the trail in the burn scar cavity of this huge white pine that I'd never seen before. I clipped on Cubby's leash and tried to get him to come out, but he wouldn't. So, I climbed inside with him." She paused, gauging Peter's reaction. They were almost down the hill now, making their way back to the pond and the parking lot. He was listening to her attentively, no sign of emotion on his face. She took a gulp and forged ahead with her story. "It was like a force field held us inside the tree, and the tree was communicating with us. It's hard for me to explain, but the tree showed me what it was like to be a tree. There were three scenes and three concepts the tree seemed to want to communicate. The first scene was a memory of my late aunt and me walking the trail and commenting about how there was no acorn crop that year."

"Oh yes, I remember that year," Peter said.

"My aunt thought maybe the weather was bad for acorn production, but she wondered that it seemed to affect every tree—as if they could communicate with each other."

"It was strange, but not that unusual," Peter said. "Trees often go through boom-and-bust cycles with their nut production. It takes a lot of energy for them to produce a crop, so they can't always do it every year. They need to save up for it. But we still don't understand how all of them coordinate their schedules as a collective. It's a mystery."

Encouraged, Sheila continued. "The tree sent me a clear message: only one word, and it was 'protest.'" She didn't dare glance back at Peter now, for fear she'd lose her nerve.

"Hmmph."

"Then I saw a scene that's happening now, not far from the park. The owners of our neighborhood shopping center are clearing land for apartment buildings. The tree conveyed to me that the cleared trees were like deaths—like a massacre happening to the forest. It sent me the word 'enough.' Then the last scene was of my own church a few blocks away."

"Is that the Unitarian Church near the university?"

"Yes. Workers were clearing out some storm-damaged aspens that blocked the view of the church from the road. The white pine showed me that the aspens were screaming." Sheila paused, collecting herself. They had reached the pond, and Peter motioned her to sit on the bench that overlooked it. The bright sun sparkled white on the wavelets in the pond.

Even though the bench was large, Peter sat near her, his thigh just an inch or so away from hers. Sheila could feel a frisson of electricity in the space between them. Peter looked intently at her through his glasses. Other than his fixed gaze, his expression was impassive.

Nearing the end of her story, Sheila felt the urge to continue despite not being able to gauge exactly how Peter was reacting. She regarded him just as intently. "Trees can *feel*, Peter. The white pine let me know that trees can feel pain just like animals can. It sent me the word 'help.' The trees need our help. They need us to help them live and to stop cutting so many. They can think and feel and breathe. We need to stop treating them like we have. It's so bad for them, and for us." Sheila stopped talking, sure that her potential job with him and chance at a PhD were on the line because of her speech. Her inability to read him unnerved her.

Peter turned and surveyed the pond. Light from the water's reflection swirled across his face. After a few moments, he scrutinized Sheila and started to say something, but then seemed to think better of it and stopped, as if part of him closed off.

Sheila began slowly dying inside.

Finally, Peter spoke, still looking out over the pond. "That's an interesting story. If I were you, I wouldn't tell it to too many people." He rose from the bench and began walking toward the parking lot. Sheila followed, not knowing what else to do. "I'd still encourage you to apply for the research assistant post," he said over his shoulder as he got into his car.

Those were their last words to each other for the day. As Sheila drove home, a million thoughts swirled through her head. What had Peter been about to say? Why did he stop himself? He must not have thought she was too crazy—he still wanted her to apply for the job. Peter was a mystery. But was he one she wanted to solve? She needed more time to sort things out.

ON A SATURDAY, ABOUT A MONTH LATER, Sheila gave her parents' side door a perfunctory knock. She knew her parents wouldn't answer. They were expecting her and were probably watching TV or finishing lunch. She had left Cubby at home, due to her mom's unstable legs after her stroke.

Sheila opened the door to their white bungalow and traipsed across the yellowing kitchen linoleum into the living room. A public television show about Antarctica was on TV. Ralph and Nancy sat on their brown suede couch, close to one another, enrapt in the show.

When she saw Sheila, Nancy arose, leaning to the left as if she were fighting a strong wind. Her stroke had affected that side, but she was much straighter than she had been a few weeks before. Sheila noticed her mother didn't need to use her walker now. Her curly gray hair was a little flattened on the left side of her head. She must not have bothered to brush it when she woke up.

"Hey, Mom." Sheila gave her mom a hug. "Hi, Dad."

Looking through the space above his glasses, her father gave a quick nod, then returned his attention to the television.

Sheila and her mother walked into the kitchen and sat at the table. "I'm so glad you could visit," Nancy said. "We could really use some groceries. Would you have time to do that for us?"

"Sure, Mom." Sheila dug a thin notebook out of her purse, along with a pen. "What do you need?"

Nancy went through a long list of food. When they were finished, she got up and went to the refrigerator. "Can I get you anything—juice or tea perhaps?"

"Some OJ would be great," Sheila said.

As her mother poured them both juice she asked, "Anything new with you? How's work?"

"Work is fine. But I don't plan to stay at the library much longer."

Nancy's face paled. With furrowed brow, she asked, "Why, is something wrong? Did you get fired? You're not moving, are you?!"

"No, just the opposite." Sheila had carefully worded her explanation to her parents in her head beforehand, striving for a way to not make them feel threatened. She saw she was already too late. Quickly, she said, "I know that you and Dad depend on me, and I'm not going to desert you, okay?" Then she went on to explain how she met Peter by researching a question about trees and how he had told her he was advertising for a botany research assistant.

"Well, why did he think you were qualified?" Nancy asked, not looking reassured.

Sheila knew her mother didn't mean to be condescending. She was in shock, and this was outside the box of Sheila's library job. She took a deep breath. "Well, scientific research isn't that different from library research. I know how to find information and apparently, as Peter and the search committee said, I have a scientific mind."

Sheila reached across the table, putting her hand on her mother's good arm. "And don't worry. I don't need to move. My job will be right in town. It will actually be closer to my house than my library job. I could even walk there if I wanted."

Her mother still didn't look so sure.

Just then, Ralph walked into the kitchen. "What's this I hear about you getting a new job?"

As he sat at the kitchen table, his expression was guarded. Sheila filled him in. "And the really cool thing is I can take university classes for free with this job. All I need to pay for is the books and fees."

Her father asked, "And are you thinking of furthering your education?"

Sheila fought the old urge to say that of course, she'd never want to further her education—do something that would upset the status quo. The old trapped feeling started to weigh on her. But she wasn't going to back down, no matter how nervous it made her parents. "I'm considering it," she said.

Her father stared at Sheila over the top of his folded hands. "And how stable is this job—is it worth giving up your library job?"

Sheila squirmed under the scrutiny but didn't budge. "The professor has funding for three years for my position, but I'm sure he can get more with some other grant in the future. He's head of the department, and he has a good track record.

"Even if it doesn't work out, I will still always have my library science degree. I could always go back to working in a library."

Her mother sat back. "I don't know, sweetheart. It sounds rather risky."

Before her father could add to the negativity, Sheila said, "Look, thanks to Aunt Miranda I don't have to pay rent. I've got a decent chunk of savings in the bank. This is a chance to further my education in a field that holds my interest. I've already agreed to take the job. I start in two weeks."

Ralph cleared his throat. "Well, it's your life. Just remember, we barely have enough to support ourselves. If you get in trouble, you're on your own."

Sheila was tempted to get up from the table, say 'Thanks for all your support,' and leave. But she knew she couldn't. These were her parents. They'd never had many breaks in life. They couldn't imagine Sheila having any either. She pursed her lips and handed her father the grocery list. "Anything else you want me to add, Dad? I thought I'd go get the stuff now."

Ralph glanced at his wife and then back to Sheila, a tiny sparkle lighting his eyes, their argument forgotten. "Get some chocolate chip cookies. Not the packaged kind though, get them from the bakery. Those are the good ones." He handed the list back to Sheila.

"Oh, Ralph!" Nancy said.

"Okay, Dad. You got it." Sheila arose and walked out the door. On the side porch she paused, collecting herself. The encounter had been about as uncomfortable as she had expected. But it was over for now. She'd get those cookies as a peace offering.

HER LAST TWO WEEKS AT THE LIBRARY passed quickly. During lunch on her final day, Tina threw a going-away party for Sheila, complete with cake and balloons. Sheila received plenty of razzing for giving up her exalted reference librarian position for a new venture, but she could tell everyone was excited for her.

Surveying the table, Sheila noticed that Jason sat a few careful seats away from Tina. Tina had confided to Sheila that they'd been dating but they didn't want anyone else at work to know. The library didn't have any policies about coworkers dating, but the two figured it was safer to keep things on the down low for now. With the looks Tina and Jason exchanged, Sheila would have known they were dating without Tina's confession. Sheila was glad her friend had found somebody.

Sheila's first week at the university was a blur. There were so many new things: policies, lab procedures, computer software to learn; journal articles to read and people to meet. She watched Peter for clues about how he felt about her "tree confession" as she came to think of it. He remained maddeningly secretive until her second week on the job, after they visited the Birch Grove.

They were sitting on the bench by the pond again. Peter was gazing over the water, eyes squinted. "You know, I've been thinking about your research idea—the one about the books and tree pheromones in the paper. I think we should pursue that."

Excitement welled up inside Sheila. She looked out over the water, too, a small smile on her face. "That would be great," she said.

"I have some contacts at the local paper mill. They have a foundation that gives grants for the arts and sciences. I think we should write it up."

They discussed the details some more. When that topic was winding down, Peter said something that put Sheila on high alert. "I would like to apologize for how I acted the last time we were here." He turned to her, his green eyes alight. "I'm sorry I didn't say more, didn't let you know what I was thinking." He looked down at his hands folded in his lap; lifted one up as if he meant to take her hand in his but stopped himself. "It's just . . . it's just that, I totally believe what you said about how the trees communicated with you. I had a similar experience five years ago. Maybe not as direct as yours, but similar."

Sheila could barely comprehend what she was hearing. He believed her! All the vulnerability of her initial confession rushed over her. Now it was her turn to look away.

"You've had a taste of what academia is like. If I told any of my other colleagues about it, they'd laugh me out of the department. I'd become known as the Lorax or the Tree Whisperer. 'The man who speaks for the trees.' I'd appreciate it if you didn't let anyone else know what we're onto. People just aren't ready to hear this yet. Not many people, anyway. Native Americans, they might get it, or other Indigenous people who haven't lost their connection to nature. But the people in our department? Forget it!"

Sheila's heart beat softly. "Thanks for explaining. I had been wondering . . . I'm glad you understand. You don't know how good that makes me feel."

"Less alone than before, I bet." His voice was low as he looked back to her with an emerald scrutiny.

Sheila held his gaze. "Yes."

A heavy silence passed between them. A breeze riffled the pond's surface. Inspired, Sheila asked, "Would you like to see where my experience with the tree happened? It's not far from here—in Wickham Park."

A smile lit Peter's usually somber face. "Yes, I'd like that very much."

THE NEXT DAY, SHEILA STARED out her front window at the drizzle falling. Peter was going to come, taking her up on her invitation to walk in the park. She wished the weather were better, but at least it wasn't pouring. Walking shouldn't be too unpleasant.

She was excited. He had told her not to come into the office that morning—that this excursion would be work-related. Cubby stood next to her, gazing out the window, anticipating whatever Sheila was waiting for.

As a battered black Jeep pulled up, the dog started barking. Sheila said, "Enough," and trotted to the back door, pulling on her raincoat and taking Cubby's leash off a hook. Cubby stopped barking and followed her, waiting patiently while she connected the leash to his collar. Then he started whining at the back door, wanting to get outside to meet this newcomer.

As Sheila and Cubby came down the back steps, Peter was climbing out of his Jeep. He flipped up the hood on his blue raincoat and approached them, leaning down to ruffle Cubby's fur.

"Hey, what a great dog!"

Cubby reveled in the attention. Sheila introduced them and they ambled down the road toward the park. As they walked, Sheila asked Peter about the experience he had communicating with trees.

"I was on a scientist exchange with Russia about five years ago. My post was on an island in the largest lake in Europe—Lake Ladoga. The lake is huge, not unlike our Great Lakes, except this one has seals—*fresh*water seals, if you can imagine that."

"Oh wow, I never knew there were such things," Sheila said.

"The island's name is Valaam and it is part of an archipelago—a bunch of smaller islands surround it. My research station was in a nature reserve. Besides that, and some monasteries, the island is fairly wild and unspoiled. More than 480 species of plants grow there. I was helping to categorize them. Most of Valaam is covered by conifers, mainly pine. About a quarter mile away from my station was this *huge* red pine. I'd say it would take at least five people with their arms outstretched to reach around it. You could hike to the tree on a trail—it was right beside it. People would travel to the island from the mainland just to see this tree and some even would sit and meditate at the base of it."

Rain dripped off the hood of Peter's raincoat and onto his nose. He wiped the drops away. "One day, about three weeks into my stay, I was hiking past the tree on my way somewhere else. Nobody else was around, and I decided to see what all the fuss was about. So, I went up to the pine and I hugged it." He paused, collecting his thoughts.

"I didn't feel anything at first—just the bark, warm from the sun. But slowly, I started tingling. The sensation started in my hands and worked its way across my arms, through my shoulders, down my torso and into my feet. It surprised me and I almost let go, but something told me to keep holding on. So, I did."

"Woah," Sheila said, softly. Raindrops fell onto Peter's cheek. She resisted the temptation to wipe them away.

"Slowly, very slowly, I got this feeling of extreme peace, like I was feeling what the tree feels. I felt connected to everything and everyone on the island—all the plants, the earth, the ponds, even the buildings." He glanced at Sheila, gauging her reaction. She gave him a nod of encouragement.

"I don't know how to explain it. I felt like I had been there for hundreds of years, experienced all kinds of weather and hardship, and I was still there, still pulsing with life, and just so . . . *connected*. It was like the tree was showing me what it was like to be a tree, to be part of a larger whole. After that, I didn't think those pilgrims who performed ceremonies at the base of it were so crazy," he said. "You've probably noticed the tattoos on my arms—I got those on Valaam right after that experience. There was this tattoo artist on the island. People came from all over the world to see him—kind of like that tree, come to think of it. He was renowned for his artistry."

"I think they're cool," she said. "Unusual."

"I guess I wanted to commemorate the experience—the connection. I've been hoping that something like my experience with the tree on Valaam would happen again, but it hasn't. I think it's great that you had your experience so near your home. I can't wait to see your tree."

Sheila tugged on Cubby's leash. He had stopped to sniff a thimbleberry bush and she felt an urgency to get them to the tree. As they walked, she said, "I've felt that peaceful feeling, too—in this forest. Not so much the feeling of connection, though." She wished she could experience that feeling of peace and connection with a person, too, at least once in her life.

On their way, they discussed whether tree pheromones could be influencing people as well as other plants. They talked about the book *Braiding Sweetgrass: Indigenous Wisdom, Scientific Knowledge and the Teachings of Plants.* They had both read the book and found the insights it offered into botany astute. Peter confessed that, like the book's author, he thought of a tree as a living being; a "who," not an "it." But he needed to be careful of his language when he was around other scientists.

Sheila told him she had started thinking about trees this way, too.

They also discussed recent news reports about the Biosphere 2 project in Arizona. A college student on a tour inside this self-contained mini-Earth had disappeared, leaving behind only his shoes, and those had been found in separate sections of the facility. The science world was abuzz about the mystery. The police didn't know what to make of it.

At the turnoff to the tree, Cubby sat and whined, looking up at Sheila. "It's okay," she said. "Let's go."

The three of them tromped through the wet underbrush. Soon, the old fire-scarred white pine was in sight. Peter stopped. "Wow, that's one heck of a tree! It seems like it's been through a major fire."

They approached it slowly, carefully. At last, they stood in front of the blackened cavity. "Do you want to go in?" Sheila asked.

"I will if you will," Peter said.

"Okay. I'm going to take Cubby, too. It will be tight, but I think there should just be enough room for us all." She peered at Peter for reassurance, and he gave her a nod. Sheila fought the urge to hold out her hand for his. Instead, she beckoned him, and they entered the tree together.

They crouched down and turned, facing the opening. Cubby sat on the outside of Sheila, next to the tree wall. Nothing seemed to be happening, so Sheila said, "Let's touch the tree." They each reached out and pressed a hand against the rough black inner wood.

Slowly, oh so slowly, Sheila's hand started to tingle. As the sensation passed through her, she reached for Peter's hand. She had an image of the energy passing through him and back into the tree, creating a circle.

Peter turned to her, a smile spreading across his face. "Feel that?" he whispered.

It was all Sheila could do to nod. The feelings and images coursed through her system. The tree showed her a piece of paper, thin and unassuming in the sunlight. The feeling along with this image was less angry and strident than what she'd experienced during her previous encounter. "Do you see the paper?" she whispered.

Peter's voice was faraway. "Oh, yes . . ."

Without sunshine, there is no tree, the tree said.

A sturdy aspen came into view. Next, a logger came and felled the aspen.

Although cutting hurts the tree, without a logger there can be no paper.

Sheila saw the logger sitting down in the forest to eat a sandwich.

Without wheat, there can be no logger.

Inside the logger's thoughts, Sheila saw his mother and father. Then she saw the tree on a truck bound to the paper mill.

Inter-be, the tree said. *The sunshine is in the paper. The logger is in the paper. The wheat is in the logger. The logger's mother and father are in it, too. Without any of these things, the sheet of paper cannot exist. Everything coexists. You cannot just be by yourself alone. You need to inter-be with every other thing. Take one of the things away, and there would be no paper. As thin as this sheet of paper is, it contains everything in the universe inside it.*

The tree's consciousness receded. Sheila protested silently in her mind—she wanted the feelings to last. She'd never tried hallucinogenic drugs but guessed it must feel something like this.

Everything in the universe is in a sheet of paper—yes! She wanted to ask if trees used paper to influence people, but this was a one-sided conversation, and the main participant was ebbing away. Sheila stifled a sob. Moving slowly, she turned her head to look at Peter. Tears streamed down his face.

As if on cue, both of them lowered their hands. But just before her fingers left the charcoaled wood, Sheila had the strangest thought: *Give of yourself. Grow roots.* She wasn't sure if it was from her or the tree.

She gasped. In an instant, she realized her problem connecting with men, connecting with her community, were problems of her own making. It wasn't that the men were lacking something or weren't good enough. The problem was with her. She was not willing to be open with them, to give of herself. Her roots were shallow because she never let them grow, never invested herself. Never committed to anyone, except for her parents. She needed to allow her roots to grow deeper, to commit to being in this place with these people—to stop dreaming of being somewhere else. To form strong connections with others and a romantic partner, she needed to be more like the trees.

Peter wiped his eyes and turned to her. "You okay?" he murmured.

"Yes. Let's get out of here." She didn't think she could stand any more deep revelations.

"I don't know if my legs will work," Peter chuckled and tried clumsily to uncross his legs. He ended up crawling out of the tree. Sheila followed suit with Cubby behind.

Peter stood and put out his hand to Sheila. She clasped it, feeling that now-familiar buzz between them. She stood slowly, but then had to lean against the tree trunk for stability.

Cubby ran off into the damp forest, after a squirrel, no doubt.

Peter let go of her hand and stood in front of her, staring deeply into her eyes. Sheila saw her reflection in his eyes, repeated as if they were funhouse mirrors. A wave of dizziness engulfed her, and her knees went weak. Her raincoat hood was down, and she could feel the rain plastering her hair against her head.

As quickly as she had realized her problems with men were nearly all her own making, she now realized that Peter was the man she wanted. They had been connected inside the tree. She wanted to be connected to him outside the tree, as well. Connected for good, forever, lost in all the promise of his green eyes, melded with his fear, his bravery, his caring. Together, they could help the trees.

Perhaps Peter felt the same in that moment. A spark lit the moss of his eyes, and he pressed his lean body against hers, resting his elbows against the tree bark on either side of her head.

Out of the corner of her eye, Sheila could see the tattoos on Peter's arms moving, pulsing with each of his heartbeats. Raindrops collected on the delicate hairs there. Were the fern frond designs growing? Melding with the tree? She could hear them scraping across the rough bark, tickling her ears.

She tensed, heart pounding, only to look into the depths of his gaze again. What she saw caused her to relax. Her body slowly melted, yielded. It welcomed the weight of him. She could smell his breath now, full of spice and heat. His lips were coming close to hers.

In the back of her mind, a protest erupted. She could hear her mother's voice saying, *This man is your boss, what are you thinking?!* But as soon as that thought arose, another took its place. Yes, she worked for Peter, but there was a much larger, more important job she needed to do. She wanted this man in her life, for life. She didn't care if she was under the influence of the experience they had just shared. Wanting him made sense to her like nothing else ever had.

Sheila met Peter's lips with hers. The heat of their connection caused her knees to buckle, but Peter held her up against the tree with the gentle pressure of his body. She'd never had a kiss like that.

When their lips parted, the only word that came to Sheila was "Yes." She heard a corresponding "Yes" from Peter. Yes, this was what they wanted. All the other stuff could work itself out later.

When Sheila was able to open her eyes, she saw a movement in the distance. It was as if the raindrops were coalescing into a shape with flowing white hair and bright blue eyes. Aunt Miranda was floating in the air a few feet off the ground. Cubby sat below her, tongue lolling.

Her aunt was smiling.

Dedicated to my dog Buddy, who died while I was writing this story, and to anyone who has been held back from their full potential.

Acknowledgments

These stories are meant as a meditation on the power of appearances to deceive and captivate. We all know people in the world who seem so cultured and urbane on the outside but who suffer from warped hearts. They make the rest of us suffer also. Although several stories arose from this dark place, my hope is they will serve as warnings and touchstones for readers. I hope the other stories will open your eyes to the magic that is all around us.

Certain stories in this collection are already dedicated to specific people. However, more of my people need recognition, as well. These include my speculative fiction writing group members Lacey Louwagie, Linda Olson, and Jim Phillips, who have reviewed all of these stories throughout the years. Sadly, Jim Phillips is no longer with us.

"A Night in Biosphere 2" arose from a short story workshop by Felicia Schneiderhan in 2021. I thank her for her rules and encouragement to write first and edit later. She also provided helpful feedback on "The Stolen Stories" and "Catfished."

"The Path of Totality" was sparked during a Lake Superior Writers class by William Kent Krueger in 2018, and later workshopped in a short fiction class offered by The Loft in 2020. It benefitted from thoughtful comments by classmates Josh Hanesack and Abby Chau. It was published in the *Thunderbird Review* (Vol. 9, Spring 2021). This Loft workshop introduced me to Karen Russell's books, which led to my falling in love with her story "Bog Girl: A Romance." I reworked it into a satire of northern Minnesota society in "Bog Boy: A Northern Minnesota Romance," and I stand in awe of her creativity and talent.

I thank musician Teague Alexy for sharing insights into his creative process for "The Shower Singer." I wrote it a few years before the COVID-19 epidemic. Spooky!

"The House" was published in *Twin Ports Terror* (Vol. 1, June 2020).

Finally, I would like to thank the students and staff at Cornerstone Press under the direction of Dr. Ross Tangedal for their close attention to this manuscript. This includes Ellie Atkinson, Sophie McPherson, Chloe Verhelst, Allison Lange, and Ava Willett. You are all bound for great things.

MARIE ZHUIKOV is an award-winning science writer. She is the author of *Meander North* (2023), a memoir in essays that earned a silver Midwest Book Award for nature writing, and the novels *Plover Landing* (2014) and *Eye of the Wolf* (2011). Marie has written extensively about Lake Superior, the St. Louis River, the Boundary Waters Canoe Area Wilderness, and the Superior National Forest, and she currently works as a science communicator for the Wisconsin Sea Grant Program. She lives in Duluth, Minnesota.

www.ingramcontent.com/pod-product-compliance
Lightning Source LLC
Chambersburg PA
CBHW031601310726
48974CB00003B/767